A Royal Ending

Adventures on Brad Book 9

by

Tao Wong

Copyright

A Starlit Publishing Book
Published by Starlit Publishing
PO Box 30035
High Park PO
Toronto, ON
M6P 3K0
Canada

www.starlitpublishing.com

E-book ISBN: 9781990491412
Paperback ISBN: 9781990491405

Books in the Adventures on Brad series

Contents

Chapter 1

In the royal capital of Brad, Warmount, there exists a party of Adventurers graced with both fortune and fate's merciless gaze. For this party of Adventurers had gained royal favor, a favor that saw the third prince of the kingdom joining their ranks under the pretext of *understanding the common man and making his way without the aid of his parents*.

A common enough desire, though when expressed by a prince, engendered a series of noble plots and machinations. Drawn unwilling into the world of lordly intrigue are the members of the party. The original trio of Daniel Chai, an ex-Miner turned Adventurer with an Erlis-Gifted ability to heal even the most grievous wounds, at the price of his own memories. Asin, a member of the minority species of Beastkin that survived amongst the majority-human rule, her bestial, cat-like features gifting her speed and agility but also, marking her as other forevermore. And finally, Omrak, son of Losin, the large Northerner teenager who neared his twentieth birthday away from the sheer mountains and green pastures of his home. The team's center and tank, their melee fighter whose bravery could only be matched by his straightforward heart.

Through numerous Adventures, starting from their time in Karlak, did the three forge an unbreakable bond of friendship as they grew in strength and skill alike. Joining the original trio were others like the Healer Anne, the noble Lady Nyssa and her bodyguard Charles, and Rob, the Selkie Enchanter. Some would leave, seeking better pastures or finding the life of danger and excitement of Adventuring too much for them. Others would seek safer environs, for Daniel's unparalleled Gift of healing was as unusual as it was desired.

In the end, machinations and plots came to the fore with matters resolved in a trio of duels between manipulative nobles and the party. In the end, the party were victorious, though it came not without cost. Daniel's Gift and the Price he paid were revealed for all to know, and the party now had a pair of open slots to fill. One of which was guaranteed to include the third prince.

Months later, the newly reformed party of Adventurers were in the midst of another delve into one of the many Dungeons of Warmount. An Advanced Class Dungeon, the party is hard pressed to guard both their royal addition and survive their encounter with the murderous monsters.

***

"Fall back, damn it!" Omrak roared, ducking a hard swipe. The attacking alligator-like creature with its long, biting snouts and clawed fingers was also seven feet tall, putting even the large, blond Northerner at an uncommon size disadvantage. That he had to handle three of them, all while wielding his giant two-handed sword by himself was difficult at the best of times.

Doing so when his companions were not in position and busy attempting to draw the attention of the monsters he was fighting in the cramped room they were in just made it harder. He hissed as he paid for the lapse in attention, the alligator on his left leaving a long tear along

9

one arm, managing to slip a claw between the plates of armor between shoulder and arm.

"I have him!" Roland snapped, head down as he ducked and swiped at the croc he was chasing. The croc kept pulling backwards, dodging the enchanted weapon the third prince used, its bleeding stump evidence of what happened when the all-too-sharp sword struck.

"Erlis's tears, listen to Omrak," Daniel Chai said, head bent low under his shield as he pushed forward and struck. His hands blurred for a second, the warhammer in his hand flashing in a **Double Strike** that cracked into scaled torso and sending a resounding snap through the room. Immediately, Daniel pulled back a little, raising his shield to take the retaliatory strike, a wash of hot, half-rotten breath washing over him as the croc turned its attention to him.

"We're being flanked!" Another cry, female and noble but a little worried, carried over from behind. Daniel cast a quick glance behind, spotting movement in the shadows from the corridor that they had entered from. A single glow stone, left behind to illuminate their way was all that offered illumination. That was, until Lady Nyssa, the leather-armored mage, started casting. A sonic orb formed, escaping Mana and magic illuminating her and the area around her further and showing the hulking shadows charging forwards.

"I got it!" Charles, her bodyguard, replied. The older man drew his sword as he discarded his ineffectual bow and took guard next to his employer, the retainer drawing a dagger a second later after consideration of his potential foes.

"We need to finish this!" Daniel said, risking a blow to crack his warhammer on a swiping claw. His hammer was nearly thrown from his hand upon impact, making him regret his choice. A moment later, the croc's head ducked low, its mouth open wide as it attempted to bite his head off.

Only to rear back as a glowing, **Penetration**-enhanced throwing knife embedded itself in its throat. Another second and a flurry of throwing knives followed as **Fan of Knives** added to the creature's pain. Asin slipped pass Daniel on his right, crouched low and moving fast as her hunting knife cut at tendons and sweeping tail.

11

The fast-moving Catkin with her black skin and red cloak was a blur that shifted away from the croc, throwing knives peppering the back of Omrak's other pair of attackers.

Distraction. Enough for the Northerner to unleash a new Skill, **Deadly Blow**, to bring his weapon crashing down on a turned back. His massive weapon, using borrowed impetus and the rage that cloaked him, tore through armored scales and crashed through the meat between collarbone and neck to slide deep into torso.

A twist of his hips and Omrak tore the weapon out, leaving a giant, gaping wound and dying monster. In the meantime, Daniel used his own Skill **Perrin's Blow** to strike at his own opponent, crushing hip and sending the creature flying into its friend. Tangling the pair up and knocking them off their feet, Daniel and Omrak jumped on the two crocs to finish them while Asin scampered off to deal with their errant prince.

A moment later, their whaling upon the monsters was interrupted by the harsh screaming of the unleashed spell, a caterwauling that shook teeth and made their ears bleed; such power was embedded in the spell that it brushed pass the auditory defensive equipment they were all equipped with. For the unprotected crocs though, the damage was even worse and they fell to the ground, clutching their heads.

Easy prey for Charles and the last member of their party whose overly large war polearm came crashing down on the crocs, crushing shoulders and heads with blinding speed. He wove his attacks through the group, and when he hit too hard and the hammer head was stuck, Johan just dropped the polearm and pulled a halberd from his **Inventory** to keep at it.

Finishing up the fight, the party regrouped in the center of the chambers. Asin moved around the edges, picking up and storing the various Mana stones in a small pouch, one that was linked to the rest of the team. A simple enchantment, but it not only kept track of all Mana stones that were collected but ensured that they could all collect the pouches.

The Third Prince—Roland, as he insisted on being called—had arrived with the pouches for everyone after their first delve, handing them out with a wave and muttering how these were old pouches that none of the family used anymore.

"Where were you, Johan?" Daniel said, frowning as he looked at the Men-at-Arms. His position should have been beside Omrak or all the way in the back, covering the team.

"I. . . umm. . . well. . . I saw. . ." Johan trailed off. "Then, I fell in. . ."

"Fell in?" Daniel said with a little groan.

"Pit trap," Asin called out, waving a hand over her head from where she stood. A single pit trap, positioned just to the far left and out of the way of the fight was beside her.

"You fell into the sole pit trap in the room," Daniel said. Johan flushed and ducked his head and the Healer sighed. "Did you put more points into Luck yet?"

"Haven't leveled . . ." Johan whispered.

Of course he hadn't. Nor would he likely put his points in Luck, even if he did. The Curse he had been afflicted with was not going to be so easily swayed.

"Whatever, all right, let's talk about what happened here," Daniel said, looking around the room and ensuring it was secure. "Especially you, Roland."

"I did great, eh? Did you see how I killed that croc?" Roland said, grinning.

"That . . . wasn't what I wanted to talk about?"

"Oooh, the new blade? I did change it out. I liked the sharpness aspect I think, but I'm worried about durability . . ."

"Ummm . . ." Johan said.

"That wasn't it either . . ."

"Do you want me to get those floating lanterns then? Because I can. It really is rather dark in here . . ." Roland said, rambling on.

Daniel let out a groan, burying his head in his hands.

"Umm . . . I . . ."

"Perhaps, Your Highness, if you let our Healer—" Lady Nyssa cut-in.

"Friend Daniel is not a registered Healer," Omrak rumbled.

"Uh . . . my . . ."

"It's true. He isn't. And the Healers are getting quite upset everyone is calling him that.

They've even registered an official complaint to Father," Roland said.

"Ummm . . ."

"Just say it already!" Daniel snapped, spinning on Johan.

The nobleman flushed, looking down. Daniel's gaze was forced to follow it, only for his eyes to widen to see the swollen and broken foot.

"Shit! Sorry!" Rushing over, Daniel laid hands on it, casting his Heal Minor Wounds spell. It was a fast-acting spell, one he would normally reserve for the middle of combat to conserve Mana. But considering they were not going to be heading too much deeper this delve—again—he had Mana to spare.

Swelling started going down, the bone popping back into place with a crack, while Daniel looked up at Johan, incredulity warring with wonder.

"You climbed out of the pit and fought on that?" Daniel said.

"Uhh . . . umm . . . yes?"

"Idiot," Asin hissed, next to him. "Help."

"Ummm . . . I was trying!" Johan said.

"No, she meant we'd help you," Daniel said, translating.

Asin gave him a short nod, while Johan flushed red and looked away. He muttered so low that Daniel could not hear it and after a quick thought, Daniel decided not to ask.

Sometimes, it was better to just let things lie. Looking back at Roland who was happily chatting with the rest of the team, he sighed.

Sometimes, it was best to let things lie.

For the good of all.

***

"Four gold and seven silvers each," Daniel said, handing the funds out to everyone. The nobles pocketed their amounts without a glance, Omrak looking down at the payment with a grimace while Asin pursed her lips.

"Another great day delving! Shall we go drinking?" Roland said, grinning. A short distance away, a pair of armed guards stood, out of the way and as unobtrusive as they could be. Once they exited the Dungeon, these guards had appeared, shadowing the group.

17

"The King's Arms?" Lady Nyssa said with a half-smile.

Daniel winced, making Roland turn and frown in concern.

"What is the matter, Daniel?"

"We only made four gold," Daniel said.

"Exactly! We should celebrate."

A low rumbling sound from deep within Asin's chest rose up. Roland smiled at the Catkin. "Do not worry, they have been spoken to. The waiter was fired and no one will bar you or any other noble Beastkin from dining at the King's Arms again."

"I think, Your Highness, that it is the fact that we only made four gold that concerns Friend Asin," Omrak said.

"I . . . do not understand," Roland said, blinking.

"Ale is a silver a piece, Your Highness," Omrak pointed out.

"Is it? I never noticed," Roland said, shrugging.

Another, deeper rumble from Asin. Daniel looked over at her worriedly, and she stared back

at him. Unspoken words passed between the pair
before he sighed.

"Your Highness . . ."

"Roland. I might not make the Northerner
call me properly, but you surely can!"

"Roland. We only made four gold from our
delve today. Drinking at the King's Arms is
expensive. As is living in the city itself. Repairing
our weapons, food, and savings. It all costs. We
also should practice our team coordination
further," Daniel said.

"You mean when I broke away," Roland said.

"Yes," Daniel replied.

"I know. I'm sorry. I shouldn't have. I just
got so excited and knew you guys could handle
the other three," Roland said. "I promise to do
better."

Asin let out a little chuff, recalling the other
times he'd promised.

"It's not about promising. It's training so
even if you do break away, we can cover for you
when necessary," Daniel said, lips pursed.
"There are times when you charging ahead is
necessary. But we aren't ready for that yet. We

need to train together, so you don't break away. And if you do, we know."

"Well, of course we should train," Roland said, nodding.

"Then—" Daniel began.

Roland, however, kept talking, ignoring the fact that Daniel was saying something. "But we should also rest. My previous groups always delved one day and trained another."

"Then we will train tomorrow and train the whole day, shall we not?" Lady Nyssa said, cutting and smiling at Daniel while giving him a look.

"Ah . . ." Roland hesitated.

"What?" Daniel snapped. Out of the corner of his eyes he noticed how Lady Nyssa flinched, as did Johan. He did not care, frustration bubbling through him.

"Oh, I can't train tomorrow," Roland said. "There's this ball I have to do." Seeing Daniel beginning to scowl, he reached out and patted Daniel on the shoulder. "It's not as if I want to do it—but my father asked me to. My second brother is busy, and well . . ."

With a huff, Daniel waved his hand. What could he say when that weapon was pulled? It was not as if anyone—not even Roland—could tell his father no.

"Now, come on. I'll buy the drinks," Roland said. "Call it my apology for missing tomorrow's practice. Though, all of you could come too." Eyes twinkling, Roland leaned in and bumped Johan's elbow. "Lots of young ladies coming out at that time . . ."

"Uhh . . . I . . ." Johan blushed, while Roland, having said his piece, walked off with the expectation that the others would follow.

Lady Nyssa hesitated, looking between the group but took off after him after a second. Johan followed soon after, keeping a respectful step back, as did Charles. Leaving the original trio to stare at one another. In the end, Omrak put his hands around his friends shoulders and guided them forwards.

"Let us drink. Free ale is free ale!" Omrak said wisely.

Chapter 2

"Friend Daniel, would one save this poor hero from an ignoble death?" Omrak cried, stumbling into the breakfast room in the guild hall. Daniel, seated with a large plate of breakfast foods, smirked as his blond friend took a seat beside him, looking the worse for wear having overindulged.

"I should let you suffer," Daniel muttered, but when his friend gave him a piteous grin, he chuckled and touched his friend with his hand. A slight push with his Gift, a brief few seconds of memory, and he set his friend's body on the right path. "Go. Drink water, a lot of it. And eat well too."

Omrak was already stumbling away, knowing the routine.

"Foolish. Not teaching well."

Daniel jerked, then turned to glare at his oldest friend. She grinned back at him, having taken a seat with her heaping plate of sausages, shredded meat, and bacon with nary a sound. The Catkin looked pleased with herself, but nodded to where Omrak was creating his own plate when the Healer raised an eyebrow.

"He's young still. He'll get over the drinking phase," Daniel said, justifying his decision to his friend. "He was getting better too, before, you know."

"Prince." No scorn, no inflection even in the Catkin's words.

Daniel knew how she felt, but Asin was smart enough not to voice her opinion. As a Beastkin in a capital—especially the nobles—that looked down on her kind, she was careful not to step out of line. Already, being a Beastkin in the prince's party had put a target on her back, one that she chose to share with Daniel and Omrak by staying close to them. No longer did she disappear by herself, at least, not for the most part. Individuals looking to deal with the "uppity" Bestkin were, unfortunately, all too common.

"Yes," Daniel sighed. "I guess we're alone today." The Catkin nodded. "Training again?"

Asin shook her head, and fished in her tunic for a second. She extracted a piece of paper and dropped it off with Wu Ying, leaving him to pick it up and read it over.

"Huh. And that's today?" Daniel said.

23

Another nod.

"It'd be a nice change of pace . . ."

"What would be, Friend Daniel?" Omrak rumbled. Then, spotting the scrap parchment in Daniel's hand, he pulled it from Daniel's hand after dropping his plate aside. He stared, mouthing each word as he read before looking up, smug in his hard-trained skill. "A quest!"

"An assignment," Daniel corrected. "It'll be dirty and squashed and we won't find a lot to fight. Maybe nothing at all."

"Minimum."

"Exactly, Friend Asin. There is a guaranteed payment," Omrak said around a mouthful of bread and sausage. He gulped the mouthful, taking another bite before he continued. "We certainly need the funds. And who knows, we might be lucky. It'd be about time for a change!"

"Omrak, manners, please," Daniel said, quietly correcting his friend.

"Bah! The vice-guildmistress is not here. I am allowed to eat how I will. All these nobles and their—urkkk!" Omrak spluttered to a stop as his ear was grabbed from behind and twisted. He stretched and half-rose as his assaulter leveraged him up.

"Oh, but I am here, Adventurer Omrak," Lady Marshall, vice-guildmistress of the Seven Stones Guild murmured, leaning down to softly murmur into the Northerner's stretched ear. "And you promised that you would practice. Now, is the courageous son of Losin going back on his word?"

"No, Honored Lady!" Omrak wheezed, eyes rolling furiously. Daniel and Asin were hiding small grins, knowing that the Northerner had brought this on himself. They all had been receiving lessons in etiquette now that they were partied with the prince, but only Omrak had fought against it with such vigor. It seemed to offend him on some intrinsic level, the manners of nobility for Brad. "But I only promised to practice, not all the time."

"Well, I think we should change that, no?" Another squeeze and twist when Omrak chose not to answer her question.

"Yeessss!" Omrak said, relieved when she let his ear go.

When he sat back down with a thump, rubbing his ear, Lady Marshall glared at the trio. "You three have the most to lose. Yes, even you, Daniel. If nothing else, your friends could be taken. We have told you, many times. You are being watched. Act like it."

The trio grimaced in unison before murmuring words of assent and acknowledgement. Once they had finished properly expressing their contrition, Lady Marshall held a hand up, silencing them. She made a few gestures, and a slight pressure filled the air around them, forcing Daniel to pop his ears. He knew by now that marked the casting of a hasty privacy barrier.

"Now, I've heard rumors that you three are unhappy about the speed of your progress?"

"He just doesn't train enough," Daniel said, softly. "We keep having to cut our delves short because he just won't listen and stay with us. It's . . . frustrating."

"Poor," Asin added. Lady Marshall glared at the Catkin, until she reluctantly was forced to clarify. "Low coins."

"We seek not much, but glory. And in his presence, we cannot even find that, Honored Lady," Omrak added.

"Firstly, I told you, we're Adventurers. There is not hunting for glory among us, just coin," Lady Marshall said, leveling a finger at Omrak. The Northerner quailed before the pointed finger, before she turned to the other two. "As for you, Daniel—just because you and your friends have always been training maniacs does not mean everyone else is. Most Adventurers do not enter the Dungeon every day or every other day, spending the rest of their time not in the Dungeon training. Most choose to have lives." When Daniel made to argue, she continued to speak, rolling right over his words. "And taking time off to spend working in local hospices and clinics is not counted as a break.

"Accept that the prince is a more typical Adventurer. He will train, he will progress—if not, his father would never have accepted him becoming an Adventurer at all—but he will not be following your schedule. He has, justifiably, other important duties to attend to."

Daniel grimaced, but eventually nodded in acceptance. Of her words at least, if not the reality. That might take longer.

"As for you"—Lady Marshall paused as she turned to Asin, then smiled—"Well, you have a point. The city is expensive, and while we are covering your stay in the guild's quarters, Adventuring is expensive. And having a prince in your midst should have some benefits. It just took us a while to come to an agreement."

A hand reached into her robe, and three coin pouches landed on the table. Asin snatched up the first, pulling it open before her eyes, cat-like and large normally, widened even further, giving her a comically adorable visage.

Daniel chose to stare at his friend's reaction for a second, savoring it, before he too checked the contents on the pouch. Only to find himself mimicking her reaction.

"Those are platinum coins," Daniel whispered.

"Yes. A monthly stipend." Jaws dropped, before Lady Marshall continued. "Also, we've agreed to allow you each access to the guild's armory to procure a single item at our expense. Within reason, of course."

"All of us?" Omrak said, disbelievingly.

"Just you three. The ones who lack . . . connections . . . to make up the difference in equipment," Lady Marshall said. "That is our own contribution."

The three grinned, sharing a moment of joy, though Daniel felt a little guilty. Just a bit. He knew that for the others—barring Charles—the addition of the prince was offering other, ancillary benefits to their Houses and thus, offering them further access to their Houses' own armories. Even Charles had received new equipment as his own role had expanded. And Daniel had spotted the man wearing better and new tunics recently, likely the result of an increase in his base salary.

"When can we get them?" Daniel said.

"Mmm . . . in a few days. Opening the armory is an elaborate process, so you'll have to be patient," Lady Marshall said. "You will be informed beforehand once we know for certain." Once more the group nodded. "One last thing."

A hand came up, this time clutching a necklace of delicate gold and silver filigree, with runes etched on the intricate braid that cradled emeralds and rubies and a single, large Mana stone. It was a beautiful and quite feminine piece, which was why Daniel was surprised when the Lady pushed it towards him.

"Wha—t?"

"This is for you to wear," Lady Marshall said. "Taken from the Royal Treasury itself, it is an Artifact of great power."

The trio froze at the word Artifact, none of them daring to even breathe as they stared at it. Artifacts were as different from standard enchanted gear as a copper coin was to platinum. There was no true comparison, and few Artifacts were created each century. Most were made by demented and gifted craftsmen, their lifetime Masterpieces.

"What does it do?" Daniel said, still not daring to touch it.

"It helps to reduce the Cost of your Gift," Lady Marshall said. "And before you ask, we're not entirely certain how. The Artifact has not been taken out in centuries, and records of its exact workings have been significantly eroded and uncertain. It is hoped that you will report in more detail."

Daniel gulped and took the Artifact. Even dreading the responsibility of owning such an item, he would not turn down the gift. Or bribe, depending on how you saw it. After all, the Price he paid was all too high, with portions of his life stolen each time he used it.

Sliding the necklace on and slipping it under his shirt, he felt a surge of power enter his body, the Artifact attaching itself to his aura and himself. Somehow, he knew, it would not come off now unless he willed it.

"Now, that is all that I had to do with you. Is there anything else you would like to raise with me?" Lady Marshall said, the tone of her voice warning them that there better not be. The group shook their heads in negation and the vice-guildmaster strode over, disappearing out the doorway soon after.

Silence fell over the group, before Asin tapped the table with one long claw to draw their attention. Once she had it, she was succinct as always.

"Quest late."

Hurriedly, the pair still with food on their plates ate at the pointed reminder. Newfound wealth or not, they—Asin—had agreed to the quest. Failing to follow through would see them penalized by the Adventurers Guild. And nothing, not even royal edict, would save their reputations if they failed too many quests.

Anyway, money was not the only reason these three Adventured.

***

"This reminds me so much of Karlak," Daniel said as he edged along the caverns.

The entire delve had reminded him of his time in the Beginner Dungeon. First, going through Warmount, they had travelled through manufactured hallways down the fortress itself, plunging deep into the bowels of the stronghold that had been carved and situated on the mountain itself. Then, once they passed the manufactured lands, they entered these natural stone caverns, struggling through tight corners and climbing up tight walkways.

"Yes. Familiar," Asin said, her voice echoing down the tunnel. Then, she added, "Shhh!"

Daniel wanted to chuckle but kept it to himself. He knew any noise they made, even the low murmur he had used initially was something that would echo through the tunnels. But the entire point of coming down these tunnels was to find monsters and, most importantly, sappers.

One of the greatest threats to Warmount—the Master Class, deeply entrenched and multiple quest line Dungeon they were within—was the danger of sappers. Periodic sweeps of the lower levels to find and kill such generated attackers was a necessity. Of course, fighting in tight quarters like this was not the preference for most Adventurers—the lack of support and the altered fighting techniques one needed was unusual for most.

Which was what it made perfect for the Karlak graduates like Daniel and his team. Of course, the fact that the extensive cavern system beneath the mountain meant that finding such

33

sapper parties was difficult was also why there was a minimum payment amount, one that was pooled from and paid out by the Guilds attempting to "win" the latest iteration of the Master Class quest.

Silent now, the group made their way through the caverns, dressed down to lighter armor and fewer weapons. Daniel had his shield stored, a smaller buckler in hand and his hammer by his side. Omrak, wearing only his tightly belted, enchanted, soft-leather armor had stored his greatsword and was wielding the paired enchanted hatchets he carried. Easily usable to throw or cut those who closed in on him, the weapons were a favorite mid-range solution for the big Northerner. Only Asin had foregone changing her equipment, having always worn light armor and wielded her knives.

It was nearly towards the end of the day when the group finally came across the first signs of their prey. It was not their first fight—the Dungeon spawned minor Dungeon monsters deep within the caverns like Kobolds, enchanted Rock Beetles and Venomous Caterpillars, but none of those were a real concern for the experienced party.

However, the patrol of Korrigan and the single Grendel that accompanied them was another matter. The Korrigan were small, dwarf-like creatures, standing only four feet tall and slimly built. Daniel knew from reports though that they were uncommonly strong and the oversized jaws hid sharp, powerful teeth that were used to crush armor. Once a Korrigan clamped down on you with its mouth, it was difficult to make them release. Most Adventurers had to do it after they had killed the stubborn, pupilless creatures.

As for the Grendel, it was as big as the Korrigan were small. Dwarfing even Omrak, the creature was eight feet tall of corded muscle and slimy skin. Its presence down here was unlucky for the team, and though it might seem at first glance that its large size was incongruous to be in such tight places, those individuals did not know of the Grendels' strange ability to contort and squeeze their bodies through even the smallest openings. So long as its head could fit, the monster could squirm its way through.

Asin, spotting the group first, signaled the team to a halt. Then, using a series of hand signs, informed the waiting pair of what she saw. Turning her head to see her friends, she continued the conversation.

"*Plan?*" she signed.

"*Big. Mine,*" Omrak returned quickly, a gleeful smile splitting his face.

Daniel rolled his eyes a little, but then ran a hand down his armor. He pulled out a small glass orb, a similar contraption to what their old Enchanter member Rob had used and showed it to the others with an inquiring eyebrow raise.

Nods from them around and Daniel added a few other quick command details. "*Orb first. Three count. Asin and I, Korrigan. Pull group away. Omrak, after pull.*"

Once the pair acknowledged the simple commands, the trio put the plan to action. There was no long planning session, partly because the team had worked together for so long, they understood their places in battle and partly because they feared being found out. All too often, such patrols would move on, and an inadvertent accident could easily alert them of their presence. Never mind potential other tragedies like a second patrol or a roving monster appearing.

No, faster was better. This was why they trained beforehand anyway, outside in the guild halls, so that they understood what they had to do. Now, if only they could convince the prince to put more time in and follow the formations.

Daniel shook his head violently, dispersing the thoughts and finished the silent countdown. He stepped to the side, briefly coming into view as he lobbed the orb at the monsters underhanded. One of the Korrigans spotted him, beginning to shout a warning, only for Asin's thrown knife to lodge in its throat, cutting it short.

The other monsters still noticed the problem, but it gave them enough time. Time for the team to duck back around the corner of the passageway, for the orb to impact the ground and shatter and for the energy contained within to release.

A combined shrieking and light display erupted, stunning the monsters in the chamber.

Daniel had a second orb that layered targets with a sticky web—derived from another nearby Dungeon monster—but this was more appropriate. The Grendel was too large to get caught, and the team wanted to pull the Korrigans away.

Daniel, after the initial shriek of noise, ran in, his small buckler in hand and hammer coming down hard. It crushed one head, leaving a sizeable impression and on the backswing, lodged its spike into a raised arm to yank the opponent off-balance.

Throwing knives, glowing with power and replicated, showered the caught monsters. Asin burnt through her Stamina to use **Fan of Knives** in quick order, and Daniel chose to follow her example, using **Perrin's Blow** to send one monster flying into another before he retreated.

Already, the Korrigans were recovering and swiping at him, forcing the Adventurer back. A couple moved towards Asin, intent on closing on the Catkin while the Grendel roared, wanting to push through to attack the other two but caught behind its friends.

As the Adventurers retreated through the small cavern that hosted the patrol, they directed the group's attention away from their initial starting spot. Unfortunately, the impatient larger monster chose to ignore waiting for its friends, instead throwing its own allies aside as it pushed forward.

"Ba'al's favor," Daniel swore. He caught a swing by the large monster on his shield, sharp claws raking the front face and staggering him backwards. The monster was huge, its strength formidable. As he recovered, one of the Korrigans managed to slip in, stabbing him with the shiv it used and pulling it away, bloody.

Before the rest of the monsters could capitalize on the action, Omrak struck from behind. He chose to trigger his new attack **Grand Sweep** that struck multiple targets at once. It was less effective without his greatsword, instead putting the Northern into a dual-wielding spin, but it did manage to kill one Korrigan and injure the Grendel.

Unfortunate for Daniel but the Grendel did not seem interested in changing targets, even struck from behind as it was. It kept attacking

39

Daniel, swinging his arms at the Adventurer with each strike. Rather than just take the damage, some of which was being healed by his own **Healing Aura**, Daniel occasionally triggered his **Flawless Dodge** skill proficiency, managing to somehow avoid attacks by the barest inch. It always set him up to counter, though more often than not, he'd use it against of the Korrigans that tried to flank him.

A **Shield Bash** sent one Korrigan bouncing backwards, leaving Daniel space to step sideways rather than back. An important move since he was fast coming up to the end of the cavern. Being trapped with his back against a wall was fine against numerous and weak enemies, but against the Grendel, it was just a recipe for disaster.

Hectic moments passed, the Korrigan squad whittled down by Asin and Omrak till the pair could turn their attention to the final Grendel. By that point, Daniel's arm ached, his shoulder and even his chest bruised from repeated strikes, some of which had compressed his shield all the way into his own body. But he had managed to hold on, which was all the pair needed.

A **Penetrator** jumping blow allowed Asin to put a blade directly behind the skull, staggering and critically injuring the Grendel. As it sagged to its feet, Omrak released a lightning charged **Thundering Strike** with his hatchet, driving the blade of the axe through ribs to shock the creature's heart.

The Grendel collapsed, twitching and insensate. A quick series of strikes finished it off, leaving the team the only survivors in the arena, Mana Stones glittering on the ill-lit floor.

"Well, that could have gone better," Daniel said as he leaned against the cavern wall, his shield hand hanging down by his side.

"Ah, you are too modest. We are alive, and our foes lie glittering before us. Rejoice, Friend Daniel!" Omrak said.

As much as Omrak praised their abilities, Daniel did note how the big Northerner had come closer, making use of his **Healing Aura** to help close the few wounds he had received. Asin, being smarter and more avaricious had left them alone, picking at the Mana stones, knowing that Daniel's aura would catch her anyway.

"Now, if we could only repeat that with the rest of the team."

To that, even the positive Omrak had nothing to say.

Chapter 3

Six hours later, a group of very tired Adventurers crawled out of the depths of Warmount. Twice more they had met groups of monster sappers, all attempting to subvert and ascend the very same chambers the team had used. If not for the labyrinthine structure of the caverns below, they would have arisen after tunneling their way in, but as it was, many were caught, wandering in circles.

The team had not only found and fought such monsters but also located a total of three new routes. One, Daniel's mining experience allowed him to take down with a few strategic blows to supporting beams. The other two, the group just marked on their maps, knowing that specialized teams would be sent to deal with them later.

Their ascent and the ground the team covered was significantly faster than most others; Daniel's **Mapping (II)** function offering the group unparalleled mapping abilities, even deep underground. The Healer had to admit, even if he was not the best up-front fighter, his utility as both a Healer and ex-Miner had significant advantages for the team. At least in a situation like this.

He doubted any of that would be that useful patrolling the walls for example.

"Very nice. I swear, you Karlak graduates are the best at these things. Must be all that crawling through tunnels, eh?" the grinning, bearded dwarf female said, looking at the map that she had pulled from Daniel's own Skill-created one, reviewing all the information that had been provided. Next to her were the Mana stones that the team had acquired too, proof of the monsters that they had fought. "Alright, I've confirmed your story. Now, you can sell the Stones to us or to the Guild. We'll give you a small bonus if you sell it to us, say an extra silver for the big ones?"

"Illegal," Asin pointed out.

"Bah!" Jude said, leaning forwards and lowering her voice. "What they don't know won't hurt them, eh? And we got uses for it."

Daniel frowned, glancing around the spartan office. While technically illegal, the sale of Mana stones within the Dungeon was a gray area. You had to sell Mana stones to the Adventurers Guild upon exit if you were not using them for your own personal reasons—an exception carved out for enchanters and sorcerers—but they had not exited the Dungeon. So, it was a gray area for sure. Still . . .

"Ooooh, you're one of those goody-two-shoes parties, eh?" Jude said, wrinkling her bulbous nose. "I don't really like those kinds."

"I am uncertain about my feelings about you as well, Hero Jude," Omrak rumbled, crossing his arms across his broad chest.

Daniel raised a hand, stilling his friend. He glanced over at Asin, the Catkin understanding his meaning as she began to pick up and store the Mana stones immediately. While she did that, Daniel caught Jude's attention.

"I wouldn't call us that, but we've got our reasons for playing things straight," Daniel said, softly. Among other things, he had to admit, the lessons Lady Marshall had pounded into them about the entire team being under additional scrutiny was making itself known. "Now, our pay . . ."

"Just take this to our guild." Jude thrust a small rolled up piece of paper at Daniel.

Annoyed, Daniel took a few extra seconds to unroll the paper and verify that everything was correct in it before he offered Jude another bright smile. "Thank you so much. Do call on us again. We Karlak graduates do like digging holes and delving into them."

Daniel noted how her eyes narrowed as he finished speaking, but he did not wait for her to protest as he turned around and hurried off. Let her think about that. They had coin to collect and a long bath waiting for them.

***

Later that night, after they had bathed and cleaned the accumulated sweat, blood, and musk from their flesh and partaken of a significant dinner and split the coins, Daniel lay in his tiny room in the guild. It consisted of only a single bed, a table, storage chest, and armor rack, but it was more than enough. It was not as if he had a lot of goods to store, though.

"Eighty-seven platinum . . ." Daniel muttered to himself. He truly was beginning to accumulate quite a decent amount of funds. While he preferred working at the hospice and free clinics, those visits had decreased significantly. Between his duties to the guild, his training with Lady Marshall on etiquette and politics, lessons to learn new healing spells, regular Adventuring training, and delving, his free time had been squeezed significantly. Still, Lady Nyssa and Marshall still found ways to cram in a few visits by nobles and wealthy merchants that had ailments that needed his special Gift.

In most cases, he would have turned them down. However, many of these ailments could not be fixed by normal spells—or required the extremely limited time of the Grandmaster Healers. And rich and poor alike deserved relief from pain and ongoing suffering.

It did help that they provided a significant payment later, a portion of it that Daniel then dedicated to sponsoring new Healers, both from the slums and to take his place where he could not go. In some ways, the Adventurer had to admit, he was probably doing more as a net benefit just throwing money at the problem than going himself.

After all, a single healing often let him sponsor multiple individuals for months. Individuals who could then progress their own skills, growing stronger and, yes, eventually tackle even more complex diseases and injuries.

Now, if only he could get rid of his lingering sense of guilt at not being there himself.

Forcing his mind from long-worn thoughts, Daniel instead focused on his next step: his most recent Level Up.

Level Up!

Adventurer Level 29

You have gained 5 Attribute Points and 1 Skill Proficiency.

Slow as their progress was for Daniel's own desire, they were leveling. It helped that he was not using his Gift as much as before, his more powerful spells and the Healing Aura helping to fix minor issues while the higher quality of their equipment meant that injuries were lower too. It meant that for once, he was not progressing slower than his team—well, not much—which was a welcome change.

With the new Level Up, Daniel had to consider how he wanted to balance his attributes and Skill Proficiencies once more. His Skill Proficiencies were, for the most part, simple enough. He had planned on advancing his **Healing Aura** for a while now, and with a stronger front-line team that required his presence less, the **Aura** improvement would allow him to provide aid to both front-line and back-line fighters at the same time. Even if, for example, someone broke away since the upgrade would extend his range as well.

It did, however, push Daniel further from his front-line role, but the Adventurer had to admit, a part of him was fine with that. He did not have Omrak's bloodlust, nor desire for further glory. He enjoyed delving for the challenge, not the pain.

Furthermore, **Healing Aura** as an upgrade for his Skill Proficiency was an excellent choice since he would be receiving continual training from Healer Rotfield This would improve both his mundane Skills and his magic Skills, giving him new spells to wield. Even if his Gift allowed him to heal any major injuries, it was still preferred to use Mana first. A fact that even the king had agreed to which was why the lessons had been arranged to begin immediately.

Like most things, learning a new healing spell was still months away, but he could see the very real progress he was making. It would have helped if the Healer was able to see him more often and did not foist him off on apprentices, but considering Daniel was learning Healer secrets for free, he was not about to complain.

All that meant that when he came around to choosing his attribute allocation, the smart move was to pour points into Intelligence and Willpower, both of which would aid him in learning and regenerating Mana. The effects of both were, of course, subtle but marked. Everything from being able to understand concepts faster to being stronger willed and less prone to fear effects were well catalogued.

Of course, basic born abilities played a part too. These attributes both developed an individual and aided in shoring up weaknesses, but they could not, without hundreds of points in them, alter fundamental problems. A naturally feeble individual or one who had grown up malnourished would always be weaker and less healthy than a strapping farmer or a well-fed nobleman.

Attributes were Erlis's way of rewarding those who sought to better themselves. Or, as his grandfather used to say, you could chip at a rock and make a beautiful jade sculpture—but if the rock was limestone to begin with, you best not leave it in the river.

Of course, on that note, Daniel had to admit, he had a decent base to begin with. Which meant adding a few points to Intelligence and Willpower did aid him, in both study and his Mana regeneration. Still, a little Luck never hurt.

Dumping two points into each of the first two and the remainder point into Luck, Daniel flicked up his Status after confirming his new **Healing Aura** upgrade.

Name: Daniel Chai (Advanced Rank Adventurer)	Race: Human (Male)
Class: Level 29 Adventurer (11.6%)	Sub-classes: Level 6 (Miner) (0.3%)
Life: 429	Stamina: 429
Mana: 324	
Attributes	
Strength: 43	Agility: 37
Constitution: 48	Intelligence: 43
Willpower: 37	Luck: 23
Skills	
Unarmed Combat (Novice): Level 5 (197/100)	Clubs (Skilled): Level 7 (38/100)
Archery: Level 7 (47/100)	Shield (Skilled): Level 4 (21/100)
Dodge (Skilled): Level 1 (16/100)	Combat Sense (Skilled): Level 9 (02/100)
Perception (Skilled): Level 1 (03/100)	Mining: Level 3 (09/100)
Healing (Skilled): Level 8 (88/100)	Herb Lore: Level 8 (67/100)

Stealth: Level 3 (63/100)	Cooking: Level 5 (18/100)
Singing: Level 2 (01/100)	Tactics (Novice): Level 5 (78/100)
Heavy Armor (Novice): Level 2 (78/100)	Politics: Level 8 (98/100)
Sense Motive: Level 5 (72/100)	Leadership: Level 9 (14/100)
Skill Proficiencies	
Double Strike (III)	Shield Bash
Perin's Blow	Find Weakness (II)
Mapping (II)	Inventory (Adventurer Special)
Personal Armor (I)	Healing Aura (II)
Flawless Dodge	
Spells	
Minor Healing (II)	Healer's Mark (II)
Cleanse (Toxins) (I)	Cleanse (Disease) (I)
Healing: Medium Wounds (I)	Treat: Minor Wounds
Gifts	
Martyr's Touch—The caster may heal oneself or others by touch and concentration,	

> sacrificing a portion of his life to do so. Cost varies depending on the extent of the injuries healed.

As for his new **Healing Aura (II)**, the bump in regeneration and distance was nice, but it had not evolved to anything major. Not that he expected that, just yet. Still, it did mean that his presence in the guild hall continued to benefit one and all. Even when he was resting.

In fact, one of the most popular stories was a particular Healing Sage who had chosen to make his resting place on a remote island. So powerful was his **Healing Aura** that the nearby villages and the fish themselves had bloomed, creating a minor local boost in economy. Until, of course, decades later when he finally passed away.

Content with his choices, Daniel willed the status screen away and closed his eyes. Today had been a decent day. As his eyes drifted close, the ring of experience on his finger gleamed, playing memories of the day's events through his sleeping mind, providing further reinforcement of the lessons he had learnt this day. And if his sleep was a little less than perfect, well, it was just another compromise he made to keep his Gift usable.

Chapter 4

"I'm sorry, I have forgotten my lord's and lady's names," Daniel said, staring at the portly man before him. Beside him, his thinner wife sat on a couch, having been guided to it immediately upon entering, her face pale and wan while the rash across both cheeks like a pair of spread butterfly wings burnt bright.

"How dare you! We were introduced to you a month ago at Lord Oniani's ball. How could you forget who we are?" the man said, his eyes bulging in anger.

"Dear—" His wife's voice was softer, caution filling it.

"No! Peasants like him should know his place," the man said, almost going as far as to stamp his foot. Lady Marshall, standing by the door of the sitting room the group was meeting in, frowned. She stared at Daniel, who gave her a little shake of his head, though he had to swallow his rising irritation. This was the last thing he wanted to deal with at the start of the morning, but he had promised Lady Marshall.

"My lord, you might have forgotten, but my Gift has a price," Daniel said, his voice calm but stern. "I do not choose which memories are taken from me when I wield my powers. At times, such circumstances occur."

The lord paused, hesitating at Daniel's excuse. He stared between Daniel and then Lady Marshall, who stepped in smoothly.

"And I should have remembered to reintroduce you. That is my fault, and I hope the Lord and Lady Rinelt would forgive me," she said smoothly.

"Well, if it's because of your Gift . . ." Lord Rinelt trailed off. "You should hurry up anyway. We have better things to do than wake this early. Really, you should have more convenient times."

"Of course," Lady Marshall murmured. She stepped forward, placing a hand on Lord Rinelt's arm and then leading him to the side, while murmuring in a low voice. "Why don't we discuss perhaps a better time for you both, for future visits, while we allow them to speak in privacy."

"Future visits, I thought . . ."

Daniel tuned the words out, taking a seat beside the Lady Rinelt and scooting the chair closer. He offered the woman a gentle smile and got one in return. A rather sad one.

"You can't heal me, can you?" Lady Rinelt said, softly.

"No, not fully. I can ease the symptoms, but . . ." Daniel sighed. "You're the second such patient to arrive, which is why the Lady Marshall knew better."

The Lady Rinelt nodded, then turned away for a second. Her fingers fidgeted before she raised a handkerchief to her face, wiping at the sides. Daniel turned away, waiting for her to compose herself once more before he continued.

"There are certain types of illnesses where even my Gift is . . ." Daniel frowned, searching for the word. "Inadequate. It requires too much from me."

"Do you know what it is that I have? Why I suffer so?" Lady Rinelt said. "Some days, most days, it's fine. And then . . ." A wave at her face. "And worse."

"I don't. Not fully," Daniel said, frowning. "There are a number of diseases in what is taught that are similar, but I expect—I feel—it might all be similar. It's like your body turns against itself, your body harming itself." He turned his hand sideways. "When I use my Gift, I but readjust those signals. Then a simple healing spell deals with the rest. However, whatever it is that is mixing up those signals . . . it'll come back."

Lady Rinelt ducked her head, disappointed. Eventually, she spoke softly. "What should we do?"

Daniel glanced to where Lady Marshall was handling the over-protective and self-important Lord Rinelt, explaining to him what Daniel was doing before he looked back at her. "If you'll offer me your hand, I can do the rest."

A small smile, a timorous hand offered to him. Daniel took the soft, smooth skin in his and began, pushing his Gift through her.

And along the way, he felt something disappear. He caught a glimpse of it, as he willed his body to heal hers: a memory of a shared conversation, laughter. A fist fight, spitting out blood . . . a monster tearing at his leg.

Then, it was gone. As was her ailment.

***

"I don't like giving discounts," Lady Marshall said, looking at Daniel as they watched the pair, Lady Rinelt looking much healthier and livelier, leave on their coach.

"I didn't fix her," Daniel said, softly.

"No one can," Lady Marshall replied. "Not even Healer Rotfield is able to do anything, and he has one of the highest Levels in the land."

"I can," Daniel admitted. "But, I think—no, I know—the price would be too much." Lady Marshall raised an eyebrow, waiting to see if he would expand. Eventually, Daniel did. "A year, maybe more."

"That much?"

"At least." Daniel shook his head. "Whatever is afflicting her, it's one that is inherent to her body. To truly fix it, I would have to fix her body."

"And for now?"

"I put a dam in her body, a change. It might be weeks, months, or even years before she has another episode. But she will have one."

Lady Marshall nodded, the older woman pursing her lips. "If you provide me a more extensive list of such diseases or what to look for, I can ensure to decline requests from such individuals if you wish. Or at least provide you their symptoms beforehand."

"That would be useful," Daniel said, shaking off the melancholy off him. "I'll offer you the list. And . . . I'd like to continue to see them. If they'll see me, knowing I can't heal them fully."

"That can be arranged," Lady Marshall said. "Though I don't understand why some you are able to fix easily like those with the wasting thirst, and others with the same disease require constant treatment."

Daniel frowned, considering how to articulate the issue. "Sometimes, though the symptoms are the same, the causes are different. And sometimes, the causes are the same but the symptoms are different, like with the Lady Rinelt." Daniel shrugged his shoulders. "There's still so much to learn, and sometimes, I think with the spells that we use, we miss much."

Lady Marshall nodded slowly. "Well, I'll stick to casting spells. That's complicated enough for me." With a wave of her hand, she turned away from the doors and headed within, leaving

Daniel to stare into the busy morning street where Adventurers and civilians passed by.

Giving his head a quick shake, he closed the door and slipped within. If he wanted breakfast before they began training today, he best get to it. And healing always left him a little hungry.

***

The Royal Guardsman appeared before Daniel without warning, almost seeming to teleport from his position on the outside of their fractured shield wall. Prince Roland had moved forward during their clash, pulled ahead a few steps from the front of the line as he attempted to land a blow. Just enough space to open a gap for the fast-moving guardsman.

Daniel flinched, reflexively blocked the strike with his shield and being forced to his feet by the **Heavy Blow**. Omrak twisted a little, distracted by the appearance of an enemy on his flank, a distraction that the guardsman that was engaged with him punished him for, sinking his blunted blade deep into the Northerner's ribs. Breath exploded out of the Northerner's chest, even as he used the bowing motion to pommel strike the guardsman.

Or at least, attempt one. The guardsman easily parried and slipped the attack but was at least forced back. In the meantime, Daniel had little time to pay attention to the rest of the fight, a dangerous position for a Healer to be in. His opponent seemed content to chip away at his defenses, forcing the Adventurer to pay attention under his sweaty helm rather than risk being toppled or struck too hard.

The remaining team of five guardsmen took apart his own party, splitting each individual up and beating the team down in a short half minute once their formation broke. The only one able to hold his own one-on-one against the guardsmen—and only because they were holding back—was Johan himself. But once a second guardsman piled on, even the talented Master of Arms fell.

Daniel was the last one standing, since the guardsmen were careful not to damage the precious Healer, leaving him to stare at the point of a pair of swords. Throwing his hands up and stepping back, Daniel gave up and, when his defeat was acknowledged, slumped to the ground.

"Formation!" Asin, nursing a bruised thigh as she limped over to the prince, growled at him. She let out an angry chuff, her tail lashing behind her and ignoring the angry looks shot her way. "Left."

"I'm sorry, Lady Asin," Roland said, pulling his helmet off to rub at his sweaty head with one hand. He picked up his sword again and sheathed the practice weapon, making a face. "I forgot I wasn't using my normal weapon and I couldn't get back in time without the **Haste** boost."

"You shouldn't be breaking formation at all," Omrak growled, his face twisted in a rictus of pain. His breathing was coming a little short, and Daniel guessed that his ribs were bruised. The guardsmen had to hit Omrak harder than the rest of them, just to slow down the big Northerner. Thankfully, Daniel knew his Aura was busy healing his friend even now. Though . . . a quick survey of the team and Daniel threw a **Healer's Mark** on the big man, receiving a grateful nod.

"Right, right," Roland said, making a face. "I'll get it right next time."

"You said that before," Omrak grumbled.

"I know!" Roland snapped. "If you all would just—"

"We're not changing tactics to make you the spear point every time, Roland," Daniel said quietly, interrupting the prince. He ignored the looks the guardsmen gave him and the various guild spectators, all of whom were curious to watch the prince and his team train in the Seven Stones Guild's training grounds. He even ignored the way Johan flinched and shrank into himself, looking highly uncomfortable by this interaction.

"I'm just saying—"

"You have the best equipment and are geared towards that, I know," Daniel said, his irritation getting the better of him. It was three hours later and they had been beaten by the guardsmen every time. Which was to be expected—the Guardsmen were all in the 70s in terms of Levels, making them elites of elites. On the other hand, they should at least be able to hold them off for longer. "But not every fight is going to come down to tearing down a Boss Monster or dealing with a few big ones. What if we get swarmed by smaller monsters? What if we get attack from the front and behind? What if it's a lava pit with heat vents and we can't get to you?

"And never mind the fact that if you die, so do we all!"

"That wouldn't happen," Roland protested.

"Oh, you think your father is going to be very understanding if we lose you?" Daniel said and pointed to Asin. "To a Beastkin?" The finger shifted. "Or a Northerner who isn't even technically one of his people? I might survive, but Erlis knows, there's no way I'll ever be allowed to risk myself again. Which means I'd just be confined to a much slower, more broken and confused death using my Gift."

Roland face paled, while the Adventurers around chose to start slinking away. It helped that the Royal Guardsmen moved to disperse the crowd.

"You keep acting like this is a game, but it's our lives. You say you'll learn, but all you do is do the same damn thing again because you won't take this seriously. You think we want to be doing the same boring Levels day in and day out? You think I—we—chose to be Adventurers just to repeat the same thing, day after day?" Daniel ranted, waving mace and shield around. Even angry as he was, he was cognizant enough to not do that anywhere near the prince, though that forced him to raise his voice to ensure he was heard. Not that he minded.

"But—"

"Whatever!" Daniel said, turning on his heel and stalking off.

"Where are you—" Lady Nyssa said.

"AWAY!" Daniel shouted at the noblewoman, making her flinch and shrink away. Charles dropped his hand to his sheathed knife, the one non-blunt weapon he held and Daniel glared at the bodyguard before he tossed both practice shield and hammer aside and exited the arena.

Leaving behind a group of stunned party members.

"But I am trying," Roland said softly.

Asin, watching the group, let out a little amused chuff and slunk away, hurrying after her friend. It was rather obvious they wouldn't be training any more today.

***

"Angry."

Asin found Daniel stalking the streets of Warmount, just tromping through the surroundings without a care in the world. A rather poor choice, considering he had been attacked once before. Though no one had tried that recently. Still, the depths of idiocy that fools would reach were unfathomable, which was why letting Daniel move around alone was not something any of his friends would allow.

It also helped that Asin knew he probably needed to vent.

"Whatever. I'm not looking to talk," Daniel said.

"*Good,*" Asin replied in Beastkin, knowing the Adventurer knew that word at least. It hurt a lot less to speak in Beastkin than common, the words easier to form for her throat. Though, the **Healing Aura** that Daniel put out had helped, making it easier for her to talk. It still hurt, but the buildup in pain from contorting her voice box seemed to have diminished significantly. Not that she had told them, yet. If she did, they'd probably want her to join the conversations more.

The pair walked on in silence, treading their way through the streets and passing the numerous citizens of the city going about their day. Roadside vendors mixed with farmers and day laborers, servants scuttling back and forth, and the occasional housewife. Few families had the luxury of allowing their women to work from home; most of those that did took secondary jobs like washerwomen or nannies for other burdened families.

Even if Classes made work easier and the process of finishing the work simpler, the large population that powerful farmers could support still had to earn their keep. With such a large population, everything from food to clothing to space was at a premium in Warmount, which was often why individuals left for smaller border cities.

It also meant people like Asin and Daniel, in their finer clothing and weapons were an eye-catching sight. More than one civilian eyed them, some with avarice and a few with disgust at the companionable way the pair moved, mixing Beastkin and human without concern.

Still, none dared to bother them. Not only were Adventurers much more suited to a rough confrontation than your average civilian, Adventurers were also one of the largest drivers of the economy. The Mana stones that they brought back along with the Dungeon materials made for a robust economy, one that catered to their needs in particular.

Adventurer-only taverns and keeps, clothing stores, enchanted equipment, and yes, even companionship were common aspects of daily life in Warmount. Still, Daniel's passage was also noticeable for another reason—the **Healing Aura** that he put out. Small aches and pains faded as he passed by, a small change in the environment that soon had a couple of smarter strays following behind. Two cats, a low-flying raven, and a big, mangy dog.

Asin turned around and hissed at the dog that followed, but rather than scamper away, the stray just laid its ears down and growled, the tail flaring out straight behind it.

"Leave it alone," Daniel said. "It's not hurting anyone."

"*Attention.*"

Daniel paused, working out the word before he nodded slowly and turned sideways. "Ah. Right . . . I should, but . . ." He trailed off, uncertain of what he wanted. A rather common thing in his life. He liked healing people, but the **Aura** was obviously drawing attention. More than just being a pair of Adventurers would cause.

Catching sight of a swinging tavern sign, noting the crossed mace and sword beneath it, he gestured Asin to follow him. It was something he noticed that Warmount had chosen to do, a trend that he had been told was slowly catching on in other cities. A small indicator that Adventurers were welcome. Of course, such places also charged more, but generally had higher Classed Innkeepers and Cooks and better-quality ingredients to make up for it. They also—rather importantly in this case—enforced a no-disturbance policy.

The pair ambled within and after a brief, conflicted expression on the Innkeeper's face at spotting Asin, were shown to a seat near the outer wall. Daniel had requested the seat, knowing that in doing so, his Aura would peek out, leaving the animals and any others nearby a chance to benefit. On the other hand, since he wasn't by a window, it meant he had no need to see or interact with those he benefited.

Once drinks and the day's lunch—late in the afternoon still, but simmered over the stew pot—was delivered, Asin said one more word. "Angry."

"I am. It's just . . ." Daniel sighed. "I just want to keep delving. I want to see new Dungeons, I want to progress. And between the nobles and him, I feel like I'm stuck."

"Level Up. Yesterday," Asin pointed out.

"That's the first one in . . . how long?" Daniel shook his head. "And what are you now? Thirty-five? Thirty-six." A nod. "Omrak's even passed me."

"Price."

"That's what everyone keeps saying, but why do I have to pay it? I never wanted it. I just want to . . . to . . . Adventure. To fight monsters, serve the country that way. See what new Dungeons there are, test myself and keep going. Even . . ." He trailed off.

A raised eyebrow before Asin stuck a spoon of the stew in her mouth. She chewed for a second and then swallowed before reaching for a pouch by her side, pulling out a handful of peppers to toss it into the stew. She raised an eyebrow at Daniel, who nodded, taking a small pinch to add to his. After they both spiced their meal to their preference—an act that elicited a glare from the Innkeeper—they continued their conversation.

"I want to leave Brad. See new Dungeons, see the world. But . . . now . . ." Daniel sighed.

"Trapped."

"Yes." Another bite, another chew. He picked up the ale, swallowing the drink, and made a surprised appreciative moan.

73

"Agreed," Asin said, picking up her own mug.

"I did. I didn't think we had much choice." Daniel rubbed the back of his neck before adding. "I also didn't think it'd be like this."

A single eyebrow rose inquiringly.

"I thought we'd get more resources, tear through Dungeons more. Maybe he'd get bored after a bit," Daniel said. "Or be done. And we'd move on. But for months, we've been stuck. And he doesn't care and that hurts."

"*Pain?*" Asin said, ears swiveling down.

"That he's just . . ." Daniel sighed, leaning back. "I wanted this for so long, and he gets to swan in, do it, and doesn't really care. And I mean, others do that too. Not everyone really takes the business seriously. But most of those, they drop out as Beginner Adventurers."

Asin nodded, recalling all too many. It was why the both of them had been alone for so long, before pairing up eventually. Not many had the drive the pair had. Even Omrak, as close as they were now, was not a lifer. Not like they were likely going to be. He had plans, dreams of an after.

Neither one had discussed it, but this was their life. Everything they'd wanted was encapsulated in what they did now. And perhaps that was foolish, perhaps it was dangerous and prone to disappointment when they eventually had to retire.

But they were still young, and this was what they wanted.

"I'm sorry," Daniel said, waving a hand and realizing somehow, even in between ranting, he'd finished his stew. "I said I wouldn't complain but . . ."

Asin shrugged one thin shoulder, a little smile on her face. Then, big jade eyes crinkling, she motioned Daniel to come towards her. She scooted out of her chair, opening the wooden shuttered window a little and waving the man to come over. As he stuck his head out of the window, he found a sight that made him smile a little.

Cats, dogs, and beggars, all pressed up against the edge of the building, basking in the increased **Healing Aura** that Daniel put out unconsciously now. Making full use of the magic, as their wounds slowly healed and old aches and pains disappeared.

Then, to Daniel's surprise, Asin waved down the innkeeper. Using big gestures and a few well-placed words as well as the handing over a few coins, the Catkin proceeded to buy out the remainder of the Innkeeper's stew, remnant bones and scraps and stale bread for those outside.

In the middle of the commotion that the Innkeeper and his helper's exit created, the pair snuck out the back, laughing to one another. As he did so, Daniel shut down his **Healing Aura**. Making one commotion was enough. Anyway, he would do just as much good in the hospice with it on as casually blasting it around as he walked.

Chapter 5

There were advantages to being the only Gifted Healer in the kingdom. Among other things, his outburst that would have caused issues for nearly anyone else was glossed over. The next day's training went well; the prince even seeming to spend more time focused on staying with their team and holding his position than ever before. He still broke formation occasionally, but now, the word "occasionally" could be used with absolute precision.

It was during a break that Lady Nyssa came up to Daniel, facing him while angling herself away from the prince and his bodyguards. When she spoke, she kept her voice low, even as she hefted the water bottle she held in her hands as an excuse.

"You know, after you left, he stayed. All day long, practicing with his men."

"He did?" Daniel said, surprised.

"He did. Prince Roland might not seem like it, but he does take this seriously. He's just . . ." Lady Nyssa paused, then tilted her head to guzzle from her leather water bottle. "He's just not used to you. It took us a little time to get used to your team's tempo too, if you recall."

"Just a bit. And we had to adjust to you," Daniel said, recalling the training sessions they had to have when they added a half-dozen new members to the team. "Adding a real Mage was interesting."

"Yet you haven't done much adjusting for him," Lady Nyssa said, quietly.

"We have!"

A single raised eyebrow met Daniel's automatic protest.

"Fine. We could use him more, but if we let him loose—"

"He's going out anyway," Lady Nyssa pointed out practically. "Prince Roland has good instincts. A little aggressive, but his instincts are good. Against most monsters, they're the right ones. We just need to be able to back him when it *is* the time for him to break."

"And we haven't."

The noblewoman smiled a little, taking another sip and then walking off. Leaving Daniel to ponder the question.

When the group returned to the training grounds, readying themselves for another clash with the Royal Guards, Daniel raised his hand and gestured for the team to gather around.

"Okay, Roland's doing much better at holding the line. And that's great, but I'm getting a little tired of getting beaten," Daniel said, dropping his voice. "So, let's change it up on the next fight."

Omrak grinned savagely at the Healer's words while Roland puffed up a little.

"Plan?" Asin said.

"Breakout and capture. I want us to separate one of the guards and pull him so we can beat him down and take him out. Then, do it again," Daniel said. "We can't beat them one on one, but together, I think we have a chance."

"I could—" Johan began, but Daniel cut him off.

"No, we need you to keep free floating for this. I expect we'll need you to cut them off if necessary."

"How?" Charles said.

"Here's what I'm thinking . . ." Daniel said, lowering his voice further while casting furtive glances at the other team.

***

The battle had started and continued in a familiar fashion. Omrak had spearheaded the attack, using the large greatsword in wide sweeps to keep two of the Royal Guards in check. Roland and Johan had split off a little, tackling another two guardsman each while the rest of the team kept an eye on the floating fourth guard who often worked to choose when he came in, disrupting their formation. Asin's and Charles's main focus was on Roland's guard, aiding him in dealing with the much higher Leveled man and leaving Johan to duel it out alone. They had tried aiding him previously, but then the guardsmen had just turned on Omrak to finish him quicker. This tactic, of Daniel watching over them all and Lady Nyssa readying a powerful, knock-out spell, had been their best thus far.

Nothing unusual in any of that. The fact that the guard kept their attacks and their speed lowered to allow the team a chance was also not uncommon. Nor was the fact that Roland took a step too far when he was being led away, leaving a small gap that was not covered by any of the team.

What was unusual was the way Omrak chose to speed up his attacks, warding off the two other guards he fought for a few precious seconds. Even Johan sped up his own attacks, triggering **Flurry of Blades** to push his own opponent back. This was the start of a new tactic meant to help patch the gap created by Roland's movement, an obvious new addition. It did nothing for the actual space, but that was what Asin's **Fan of Knives** filling the air was meant to do.

"Get back here!" Daniel called out, angrily.

Too late. For while the series of knives flying through the air would have stopped any other fighter, the Royal Guardsmen weren't just elites, they were the elites of elites. The fourth guardsman, waiting in the wings, dashed forwards, cutting through the flying knives with millimeters to spare and appearing in the middle of the group.

Rushing to meet him were Charles and Daniel, the pair swinging their weapons and pressing the guardsman before he could cause a problem. However, Omrak was now alone, as was Roland, and it was now that they would normally begin to fall apart.

Except, Roland retreated, slotting himself back into the space he had recently vacated. More than that, Omrak shortened his attacks, flowing into a tighter defensive form while Roland and Johan took up the slack and together, the three blocked off the four guardsmen. Instead of having to manage two different guardsmen himself, now the three faced four opponents together. Even so, they would have been overwhelmed, if not for the sudden burst of energy that surrounded the team as Roland triggered a Skill Proficiency.

Royal Aura was a powerful, royalty-only ability. It was a wide aura ability, boosting everything from strength and speed to even Skills. The entire group moved better, hit harder, and in Lady Nyssa's case, finished forming her spell faster.

"Incoming!" Her barked warning was all the pair needed as they slid aside and allowed her orb to fly pass them.

The guardsman attempted to dodge aside, but at that point Charles used a new Skill Proficiency, one he rarely used. It was much less useful in the all-out brawls they fought, since **Hinder** was more of a debilitating strike. It sapped Stamina, drained energy and made the affected individual clumsy for a brief moment. The more powerful the affected, the shorter it lasted and in this case, it would barely stand for a second.

A second was enough.

The howling orb struck the guardsman, catching him in a swirling sphere of sound that rattled the jaw and shattered eardrums. As the orb dissipated, Asin appeared as if by magic, swinging her pommel down. Rather than target the gap between helmet and gorget, she used the back of her knife to strike the man. **Penetration** glowed around her hand as she struck, stunning the guardsman. A shout by a referee indicated a judged killing blow, making the Catkin grin.

Only to find herself blasted away by a rising cut that tore through her armored jacket that struck from behind, her blood splashing through the arena as it fell. The **Gale Strike** had not been pulled; the attack unleashed with all the strength and power a Level seventy-plus guardsman could wield.

The Beastkin flopped bonelessly to the ground at the edge of the arena. The entire group froze in astonishment, all but Daniel who dashed across the grounds to heal his oldest, best friend.

***

Omrak snarled, his sword coming up high and glowing as he nearly unleashed the **Lightning's Call** on the guardsmen. He only held back because the other members of the team had pulled away, disengaging while the attacker was currently being physically manhandled by Prince Roland. The Northerner fell back toward his friend, sword still in hand as he watched over the pair.

A single glance at the two was enough to inform him of the extent of damage—bad. A quick **Medium Healing** had slowed down the bleeding and begun to patch together the large open wound, but Omrak knew Daniel would not leave it at that. There was much that needed to be done, what with the armor torn open and some of it embedded in her body.

Luckily, there was no better Healer in the kingdom, especially for such catastrophic wounds. Of course, that depended on whether Daniel had the time to finish his work. His Gift was powerful, but it was limited in that it took time to work.

The group soon settled down, another of the guardsmen managing to extricate the initial attacker aside. Omrak could see it now, now that he was looking. The anger, the disdain that he showed to the Catkin. He strode off under his own power, his bloody sword still held in hand.

When Prince Roland approached the pair, flanked by the Lady Nyssa, Omrak leveled his sword towards them all. Interestingly enough, Johan chose not to approach either party, but moved further out, floating at the edge of the crowd on the guardsmen's flanks. A choice that Omrak would never have thought the timid fighter would make.

"You barbarian! You dare point a sword at our prince?" one of the guardsmen snarled, hand on the hilt of their recovered sharp weapons.

"This is not a real sword." Omrak himself was still holding the practice greatsword, though considering his strength, it was still a dangerous weapon. After all, nearly six feet of steel swung at high speed could dent even metal. When Roland shifted to come closer, he idly shifted the weapon too. "But our Honored Healer needs time to work on his friend. We would not want him crowded, now would we? Dirt and other things being kicked into the wound is all bad."

"I am just trying to check on—" Roland began.

"And you can," Omrak said, cutting the prince off. "Your highness. When she is healed."

He smiled a little, to help take the sting out of his words. Still, he refused to move, even when the guards moved closer, intent on carrying out their liege's wishes. Still, the Northerner let the simmering rage flare a little higher, letting it reach his eyes as he shifted to face the guards. He could not win, but he could hurt them.

More than that, it was time to see how much the prince's honor was worth.

"What happened to the other guardsman?" Omrak said, his voice calm. "Why is he not here to witness his mistake?" A beat, then he lowered his voice. "Or was it not a mistake?"

"He got a little overzealous, I admit. But he said he thought Asin had killed his friend."

"In a training ground?" Omrak let the incredulity show in his voice.

"As I said, overzealous."

Omrak turned and stared at the prince, his eyes meeting the others. "Do you truly believe that? A highly experienced soldier, unable to tell the difference between a blow in a training ground. Against the one member of our team that is most disliked?"

Prince Roland tilted his chin upwards, his voice growing cold. "Guardsman Griogair will be dealt with by his commander. He has been sent to report the incident himself, and will be tested for outside influence per imperial protocols."

"Protocols?" Omrak frowned.

"Rules," Lady Nyssa said, sliding into the conversation at this time. "There are rules when a Royal Guardsman attacks another, especially when royalty is involved. The entire incident will be investigated thoroughly."

"And that is all you will do, your highness?" Omrak said challengingly.

"It should be sufficient," Prince Roland said. "We have such protocols in place because of concerns of undue influence. At best, Guardsman Griogair will be relieved of his duty with me. Another individual is being sent over now."

"And will they detest our friend as much?"

"I will make sure this does not happen again," Prince Roland said, a hand crossing over to touch the griffin on his armor. "My word on it."

Omrak grunted, uncertain. Lady Nyssa smiled a little, stepping forwards and pushing at Omrak's blunt sword.

"That is the best you can expect, my Northern friend," Lady Nyssa said, her voice low so that the others could not hear. "But worry not, we'll keep an eye on Asin. And it won't happen again. Even if this was targeted, they failed."

A nod past Omrak's shoulder made him turn a little; only now did he notice the stirring noises behind him.

Asin was on her feet, being helped upwards by Daniel. To the group's surprise, it was the Healer who briefly wobbled, only to be supported by Omrak as he caught him around the shoulders.

"Sorry . . . I think I might have lost some . . . ummm . . . earlier memories. My balance will come . . ." Daniel muttered, his words fading in and out as he readjusted to the present. Unconsciously, Omrak noticed how he touched his chest where that Artifact that was supposed to help him lay. So far, Omrak had not seen any difference, but Daniel's Gift was strange and unfathomable.

Certainly for a simple ex-sheepherder like him.

That Erlis chose to Gift such double-edged boons was one reason she was respected in the

North, but it was Lundt who had their hearts. He was simple and blunt in his gifts and ire. Storms and thunder, bad weather and clear skies, there were no hidden dangers there.

Unlike this capital.

"So, what did I miss?" Daniel said as he came back. Then, as recollection fully returned, he scanned the guards. "The attacker?"

"Sent off, to be dealt with," Lady Nyssa said, gliding around Omrak now that he was distracted.

In truth, the healing was done. And if they were going to launch another attack, it would have happened now. Omrak was content to let the rest of this play out—and the lady certainly played with Daniel. Omrak noted how a hand landed on his arm, how she moved closer to him, smiling upwards.

And Daniel, being Daniel and all too moral even when he didn't realize it, was still oblivious.

"And you, Friend Asin?" Omrak rumbled, glancing at the Catkin whose claws kept popping in and out of her hands.

"Healed." Asin gave a shrug, then her nose wrinkled. "Armor damaged."

"Yes, that it is. And as apology, I'll make sure something suitable is sent for you," Prince Roland said, speaking fast. "I'm sorry about the incident. He *will* be dealt with."

"Good armor?" Asin growled, ears twitching.

"Very good. Suitable for what you choose to do. Maybe even enchanted," Roland said with a smile.

"Good."

"Good? So there are no ill feelings."

This got a half-shrug from Asin, making Omrak smile a little. The Catkin would remember. She likely would never let herself turn her back to the guards ever again. But she was also very practical. She understood how far she could push such things, being what she was.

"Now, I know we like to train, but perhaps a break?" Roland said, hesitatingly. "I'll buy . . ."

Daniel frowned, looking at the guards and the group. Omrak snorted, knowing his friend would be busy thinking of lost time, of lost opportunity. Of how much ground he had lost using his Gift. Given a chance, he would push himself to he nearly fell over, somehow thinking it would help him gain back what he had lost. Forgetting everything else that was important.

Grinning, Omrak threw his arm around the Healer and the prince, pulling them off the training ground.

"Food! Friend Asin requires sustenance after healing, and so do I. And good repast should never be turned down!"

Sometimes, Friend Daniel just thought too much.

Chapter 6

Into the Labyrinth they went once more. The center of the Labyrinth had been found by now, the Boss Chest constantly raided. There was no longer a reason to keep entering it, other than to collect materials, Mana stones, and experience. At least, for the majority of parties. There were some who still fought to be the first to clear the newly respawned Boss, who travelled deep within each day or even went so far as to camp within the Dungeon for the opportunity.

For Daniel and his team, such risks were barred from them. Not that Daniel would have taken it, even if it was an option, but the idea that they could not irked him. Even so, three dozen turns in, he had to admit, they were doing much better than ever before.

As Asin reappeared high above the skulking, Ice-Limbed Grappler, her knives extended and sinking into the creature, he had to admit that the prince's offer of the **Shadowed Armor of the Rogue** she wore was partly to be credited.

Hefting his hammer, he threw it, watching it loop through the air to catch another monster, throwing the Ice-Limbed Grappler backwards, it's multiple, chitin-covered limbs exploding backwards with the strike. The hammer kept going until both weapon and creature impacted the walls of the corridor they were in, and then with a slight gesture, it came back towards Daniel.

The **Impactful Hammer of Recall** was the Healer's own addition from the Seven Stones armory. Along with Asin's new knife, Omrak's helmet, and the rings all three wore, they had significantly increased their abilities. Of course, the other members of the party had a chance to look within, though Lady Nyssa had chosen to wait, and Charles received but a minor upgrade in a **Boots of Fleet Movement**.

"Chop, chop!" Omrak cried gleefully, having a little too much fun as blood splashed on him. He swung his greatsword up again, slicing off a limb and then another on the backstroke, the **Bleed** condition taking full effect on these creatures. More than normal, even, which made Daniel curious if they had some condition that caused them to bleed as much. "Now this is a fight worth taking!"

"Careful with that," Roland cried, shifting aside out of fear as Omrak wound up for another cut. He caught a sharp limb with his shield before he stabbed into the body. His sword slid into the monster's body with ease and then the wound itself began to smolder. A yank of his blade tore a wider wound that bled freely, even as the burn damage crept upwards.

Johan slipped between the two front-line fighters, his swords flicking out faster than the eye could see as he almost danced into the center of the fight. Both cuts finished off wounded creatures, laying their corpses to the ground where they began to dissipate even as he engaged a third and fourth. His short swords moved in a hypnotic pattern, easily dealing with the multiple attacking limbs, long enough for Charles's arrow to lodge in one long-necked throat.

Far in the back, standing by herself, Lady Nyssa watched the group fight, her hands held low and ready to cast. She never noticed the skulking Grappler that burst from the shadows, bladed legs swinging while two grasping hands moved to lock her down. Just before it struck her, a wave of sound rippled outwards from her aura, bouncing the creature backwards and sending an audible alert. The Mage turned, twitching fingers and pointing as a tightly focused **Sonic Cone** tore into the monster, rupturing internal organs and killing it after a few seconds of focused fight.

"Skulkers!" Daniel called out, noticing the attack. Movement in the corner of his vision had him throw up his shield in time to catch his own attacker, a swing by the new hammer crushing it and throwing it off. The team shifted with trained precision, altering their formation to tighten up and look out for one another.

The Grapplers might be good, but they were, in the end, just Advanced-Class Dungeon monsters. Nothing a well-organized, well-oiled, and in their case, a well-equipped team could not handle.

Grinning underneath his helmet, Daniel got to work with his team. Finally, they were clicking.

***

Outside the Dungeon, the team stretched and reveled in the fading sunshine and feel of fresh air on their faces. Even if it was noisier than ever, they could not help but delight in coming out of the Dungeon triumphant.

"Three quarters of the way into the heart," Omrak cried, throwing his meaty arms around Charles and the prince. Roland stiffened for a second before relaxing, the Northerner too caught up in their victory to notice his breach in protocol. "By the end of the week, with luck, we might make it to the end!"

"Lots luck," Asin corrected.

"Bah! We did well today, Friend Asin. Even our purse will be heavy," Omrak said.

"We did," Daniel agreed. Roland smiled at the Healer's agreement, looking happy, and then something flashed over his face. Catching sight of the change, Daniel frowned. "What is it?"

"It . . . I know we want to go on, but we hadn't planned on it." Roland paused, looking unsure for a second before straightening. "I have classes to attend to."

"Classes?" Asin sniffed.

"On geography and law, accounting and economics," Roland said. "The necessities."

"They teach you that?" Daniel said, surprised.

"Of course. How else are we to raise our skills? We're even given minor principalities from a young age to manage," Roland said.

"How young?" Asin said.

"Six."

"What?" Omrak cried. "How can that be? No child would be able to govern well."

"They don't," Lady Nyssa said in confirmation. "That's actually the point."

"What's the point?" Daniel said, confused.

"Badly run principalities," Roland explained. "We make childish decisions which affect the peasants lives, and those decisions have to be corrected. We spend our teenage years correcting them. But mistakes, along with learning why those mistakes were made, all aid Skill growth. And the correct decisions made and the experience growth from there aid us too."

"And the peasants?" Omrak said, horrified. Daniel could not help but echo his words, though only in his head.

"Are suitably compensated and knowledgeable about what will occur," Charles said, speaking up. He touched his chest, continuing. "These locations are never large, often a village at most and the surrounding lands. The residents are all sworn servants and their families, and they understand the risks." A little flicker of a smile. "It is not all bad. The noble family ensures no one starves, though lean years are possible. And the treats are amusing."

"Amusing?" Asin said, her tail waving lazily behind her as they walked. They had not stopped moving since they left the Dungeon, headed for the Adventurers Guild to turn in their Mana stones.

"Six-year-old children are often focused on simpler pleasures. I recall there being sweets on every corner," Charles said, his stern features relaxing as he recalled happier memories. On the other hand, Lady Nyssa stiffened, a flush forming on her cheeks. "Until m'lady grew up. Rabbits were considered the lord's properties, but we could hunt deer to our heart's content. Every family had to have a hutch of rabbits. Made feeding them hard during the winter."

Clearing her throat, Lady Nyssa spoke up, cutting off Charles before he could continue to reminiscence. "In any case, nobles and royalty do receive additional classes too. Having a place to practice what we learn helps sink in lessons better. Just like sparring before a delve."

Daniel nodded, the group coming to a stop before the doors of the Adventurers Guild.

"I apologize again. I know this isn't . . ." Roland paused when Daniel held a hand up.

"It's fine. You have your duties, and we had a plan," Daniel said. Learning this, and some of the responsibilities they held had eased some of the anger in him at the slow pace of their delving. It helped that all the work was finally seeming to click, especially after Asin's attack. Both their attitudes and the prince's had seen a change since then, in a small but important way.

"Thank you," Roland said, gratefully.

"Now, why are we waiting out here?" Daniel gestured inwards. "Let's get paid and celebrate! We've done well."

Silence filled the group after Daniel's pronouncement, making him turn to regard them all.

"What?" he said.

"Just that it's you suggesting we celebrate," Lady Nyssa said.

"I'm not a broken trap always," Daniel said.

"No, just recently," Omrak replied. Then, grinning, he shoved Asin forwards. "Go, Friend Asin. As said, we should be celebrating!"

Grumbling under her breath, the Catkin stalked up the stairs, followed by the rest of the team.

***

Daniel watched with quiet amusement as the Royal Guards bundled their prince into the covered and inscrolled carriage even as the slurring royal member of the family waved at them and drunkenly espoused about their individual merits. Including, in one blushing

Royal Guard's case, her very muscular and shapely legs. That would be an awkward conversation afterwards, and one that probably was better never mentioned again.

Once the prince and his guards had left, the Healer let his Gift play through his body quickly, washing away some of the toxins building up within his body and leaving him a little less drunk. Turning back into the tavern, he waved down one of the maids and mimed some beer rather than the joosh they had been drinking.

"Is he taken care of?" Lady Nyssa said, peering up at Daniel over the rim of her cup of wine. Like Charles, she had partaken, but not of the spirit. Unlike Charles, she had no significant Constitution to aid her absorption of the multiple glasses of wine, and the flush in her cheeks and dilated pupils spoke of a condition well past buzzed and into the range of tipsy.

"Yes. The guards have him," Daniel confirmed. He picked up the remnants of his mug from the wobbling wooden table, grimacing at its shoddy construction once more. For how much they paid for their ale, one would think the owner would provide better furnishings. "They'll make sure he drinks a restorative potion before he sleeps so he should be fine for his classes tomorrow."

"Good. Good. He's not a bad royal . . . just lots of burdens," Lady Nyssa slurred.

"Truth," Daniel said. "I just wish . . ."

"That he didn't choose us?"

"No. I think . . ." Touching where his hammer would normally be stored in the Dungeon, Daniel shook his head. "I'm good with that. I just wish we had more time to train."

"Yes that's—" Omrak began, only to be interrupted by the loud clomp of feet and raised voice of another coming over.

"This the prince's dogs? Shouldn't you be lapping after him?" The overly-loud voice erupted from a large warrior, still clad in his armored breastplate that was scarred with multiple cuts and still drying blood. "Go on. Shoo. This tavern's for real Adventurers."

"We are real Adventurers," Omrak said, standing up and facing the other. To Daniel's surprise, both warriors were nearly the same height and certainly similarly muscled. "Why don't you just go back and drink."

"Oh, yeah? What you going to do if I say no? Sniff my butt?" An alcohol-laced laugh burst out into Omrak's face, making the youngster flinch.

"Smelly," Catkin muttered under her breath.

"You have a problem with that, beast?" A voice near Johan's elbow made the group turn towards him with surprise. Johan threw an elbow by pure reflex, only for the speaker to slip away from it. "I thought so. Too slow. Too sloppy."

Johan turned to him, spinning on his chair. The usual hesitation, the shyness that kept the Adventurer from joining the conversation at the table in general, disappeared as he stared at the speaker. Short, hunched over, and clad in black, flashes of dark brown and green leather beneath the cloak that covered his hunched form, the speaker smirked at the Master of Arm's regard.

"Now, no need, for violence," Lady Nyssa said, smiling at everyone and standing up.

"Oh, I agree." A smarmy, rakish gentleman slipped over, catching hold of her by the waist.

"Why don't you and I have a talk? Somewhere . . . *private*."

Charles, about to block the smarmy Adventurer, was frozen as he stared at another individual, one who kept spinning a pair of blades around and around on the table. Innocuous, innocent, just another game of spin the dagger. Except, of course, his party was around the team now.

"No fighting in my tavern!" A voice rang out, the innkeeper noticing the problem. Daniel began to relax, until he continued speaking. "Not unless you all agree to **Pay for Damages**."

The Skill pressured Daniel's skin, demanding his acceptance. Before he could reject it, he felt it slide sideways, being accepted without a word as a member of his party chose to accept it for them all. A second later, confirmation from the other side of the fight—from multiple other sides—pinged off his conscious mind.

"Shit," Daniel breathed.

He never noticed who threw the first punch. He did see the first headbutt though. Carried out not by Omrak but Lady Nyssa against her gripping assailant. The poor man staggered backwards, clutching his nose at the same time the Mage held onto her own.

Without thought, Daniel flicked back on his **Healing Aura II** hoping that it would help sober the patrons. Then, a flying mug caught him in the side of the head, making him fall off his stool. Seconds before Asin launched herself off her seat over the table, claws extended to tackle another assailant.

Standing up, the Healer looked around and spotted Omrak and the loudmouth grappling one another. Grinning, Daniel stepped forward and booted the loudmouth's shin with his leg, making the man crumple. Using his momentary advantage, Omrak lifted the man and tossed him to the side.

Short-lived was the pair of Adventurers' glee at winning that minor battle, for another trio of assailants were on them within seconds. One, a low-slung and strong Dwarf caught Daniel in a charge, taking the pair of them into their table and crushing the flimsy wooden furniture. Even as the air was driven out of the Healer, he was enlightened about the state of furniture.

Lousily made furniture could be easily replaced and was less likely to seriously injure the clientele. Then, hands held up to his face, he was a little too busy fending off the blacksmith's strong wallops raining down on him from the Dwarf to worry about such trivial matters.

Chapter 7

"Fine lot of Adventurers you are!" Guild Master Ronson was berating the group, glowering at the Adventurers the next day—only technically, as the sun had yet to even rise—from within his sparsely appointed office. "Getting into bar fights, breaking the furniture, and injuring multiple other Adventurers in the brawl!"

Beside the Guildmaster, Lady Marshall was nodding along, looking entirely unimpressed with the group. "That's right."

"There were a half-dozen members of other guilds in there. Do you know the kind of messages I'm going to get? The complaints that are going to come? Do you not understand what it is like, being the party of the prince?" Ronson continued.

"It's a major responsibility," Lady Marshall interjected.

"A major travesty in our reputation! I don't even like it when our regular guild members get into fights, never mind you people," Ronson said.

His gaze swept over the team, taking in the battered appearance of everyone but Daniel. His gaze stopped on the Healer, glaring at him, but

Daniel could only shrug. What was the point of having a Gift like his own when he couldn't patch himself up? Especially when it had only required a single cast of **Healer's Mark** anyway.

Of course, once the guards and Lady Marshall had arrived to drag them around, he'd been barred from healing anyone else. Not that his **Healing Aura II** had not been running fixing minor cuts and bruises even now.

"So true. We punish our guild members for such rule breakage. And you, the prince's party, caught in a barroom brawl. The gossip that will occur," Lady Marshall said, her voice filled with horror. "A true scandal."

"Exactly. And worse, you didn't even win."

"That's ri—" Lady Marshall paused. "Wait . . ."

"If you're going to get into a fight, at least make sure to win. And make it a good win too— none of this eking-out-a-victory garbage. There were only two dozen Adventurers in there. It should have been simple!" Ronson said, fixing Johan with a glare. "I expected more from a **Master of Arms**. Or a Northerner." Again, his gaze shifted to Omrak and then landed on Asin who was still cradling one arm. "I did hear mutterings about you though, but eyes are *not* considered legal attacks in a brawl."

"Grabbed tail," Asin said, mulishly.

"I don't care if they used your tail to clean their privates. You don't try to blind other Adventurers!" Ronson roared.

Asin's ears turned down, and the Catkin gave an abrupt nod. In the silence that the guildmaster's shouting caused, Johan's soft-voiced answer was clear. "Wasn't using a weapon . . ."

"Yeah? And you think a broken chair leg isn't a weapon? Grab two of them, lay into them!" Ronson snapped.

"Guildmaster, this isn't the kind of lesson—" Lady Marshall said, raising her voice.

"And you! Why are you still clutching your head like that?" Ronson said, ignoring his vice-guildmaster as he pointed at Lady Nyssa.

"Headache."

"That's because you need to hit them higher up the head, not down at the brows. And do more exercise with your neck if you intend to

headbutt people. Wear a good heavy helm!"
Ronson advised before turning to Charles. The
older bodyguard regarded the guildmaster with a
stone-faced expression, only for Ronson to
move right onto Daniel. "And you, Healer…"

"Yes?"

"Sir, I really don't—" Lady Marshall tried
again.

"What was this healing the other fighters
garbage I heard about?" Ronson said.

"It was . . ."

"Soft-hearted garbage! You beat them, make
sure they remember their bruises. Then they
won't start a fight again."

"GUILDMASTER!" Lady Marshall roared,
her voice piercing and making the Adventurers
flinch. Asin, ever more susceptible to loud
noises, even let out a low whimper of pain as she
rubbed her ears. Still, she knew better to
complain as the furious noblewoman ranted.
"This is *not* helpful. Our members should not be
taking part in such endeavors at all!"

"Well, that's what I said," Ronson said,
wilting a little under the Lady Marshall's glare.
"But yes. No, you know, fighting. At all. Now,

go clean up and go to bed. I expect we've got a lot to deal with."

The group nodded, happy to escape the angry pair. Daniel, the last to slip out, caught the muttered words of Ronson, just before the door closed. "And win if you do."

"I heard that," Lady Marshall said.

Closing the door firmly, Daniel hurried to his room. It was after he had cleaned up the minor blood splatters and sweat from the day's delving, clad in a new tunic that knocks on his door occurred. Frowning, Daniel opened it to see Charles standing before him.

"Yes?" Daniel said, puzzled.

Stepping aside, Charles ushered in Lady Nyssa. "My lady requires your aura. Unfortunately, her room is a little too far away at the present moment."

"I—"

"Ah, Friend Charles and Nyssa, come to enjoy our favored friend's great powers?" Omrak rumbled, towel over his shoulder and his chest still bare.

"Shirt, Sir Omrak." Charles rumbled, not at all angrily but firmly.

"Right, right. I'll put it on," Omrak put action to words, and while his hand was raised, Asin slipped in underneath his arm.

"Now, come on," Daniel said, staring at the Catkin. "You're right next door."

"Muted."

"It's still good enough."

A hand came up, showing him the slight bend in it and the pair of missing claws. Yellow eyes narrowed at Daniel, daring him to say anything more and the Healer sighed.

"Whatever. Omrak, you're in the other room. Charles . . . whatever you choose."

"I shall rest outside. And you will do so with the door open," Charles said, firmly.

Daniel snorted, but did not argue. He knew better. Turning towards his bed, he groaned, noting how both women had taken it while he had been busy coordinating their rest with the bodyguard.

"I should just join Omrak," Daniel muttered, as he found an extra blanket in the foot chest and spread it out on the floor. "Teach them a lesson

. . ." Still muttering to himself, he flopped down on the ground. It really was no different than sleeping in the Dungeon. More comfortable in fact, what with the lack of potentially murderous monsters appearing out of thin air.

Within seconds of closing his eyes, Daniel drifted off to sleep.

***

Morning was a simple enough affair, though Daniel had to extract himself from the blanket that he had somehow managed to cocoon himself into. One of the advantages of running his **Healing Aura** all night was that his back and body did not ache at all, even if his sleeping arrangement had not been the best.

After kicking his friends out of his room after his morning ablutions, Daniel made his way down to the dining hall. Breakfast was subdued with the team soon breaking up afterwards to take care of their myriad duties. For Daniel, that was more lessons on healing with Master Healer

Rotfield today. Another reason why he had wanted to escape to the Dungeon.

Arriving at his classroom, he was surprised to find that Rotfield was already waiting for him. Before he could even check the time, Rotfield was already speaking.

"Late as always. Even if you are a mere Adventurer, I expect you to be on time." Having said his piece, Rotfield turned away and strode over to the front of the board. "Now, I assume you have done the reading. So we will go over the particular anatomy of the human nervous system, the way the **Nerve Defraying** spell works and how it is different from a **Greater Treat Wounds** spell."

Daniel slid into a seat with alacrity, pulling out quill—magically enchanted to always have ink so long as its user provided Mana—and paper from his inventory and scribbling the name of the spells as well as the topic.

"You did do the reading, did you not?" Rotfield barked, spinning around, a piece of chalk ready to throw at Daniel.

"I did, Master Healer."

Looking almost disappointed, Rotfield continued. "Then, list the total number of vertebrae in a human body, major differences between the major genus types in Beastkin— since you continue to insist on treating those creatures—and the names of the nerves leading and controlling the hips and lower back."

Daniel nodded, composing his mind and tucked his chin in a little, letting the chalk piece bounce off his forehead when he hesitated.

"Now, Adventurer."

Keeping his temper in check, Daniel began rattling off the answer, knowing he would see another piece of chalk coming his way soon. The books given to him had not contained details about the Beastkin at all, though some he knew from self-study.

Such were his days "learning" healing from the angry Master Healer. Even if his jealousy was proudly worn on his sleeve—at least in private— Daniel had to admit, the Master Healer's **Tutoring** Skill made a significant difference in his own Skill gain. Enough so that it was worth the abuse he received.

Hours later, Daniel was dismissed, sent to practice his new knowledge on a group of new and willing patients. In this case, they were the members of the other guilds they had fought the night before, all subjected to his **Healing Aura** and the spells he clumsily attempted to weave together.

One of the major aspects of his study was the practice of new healing spells and learning it on a manual basis, in this case **Treat Moderate Wounds**. Unlike the **Healing: Medium Wounds** spell, the **Treat** series of spells were more commonly used by true Healers. The **Treat** spells required less Mana from the caster, substituting the patient's own Mana and body resources instead and could be directed to specific locations. The **Heal** spells on the other hand bathed patients in a general aura of healthiness, which sped up healing, but of course led to things like growths and tumors.

Of course, there were other major disadvantages to the **Treat** spells such as the long casting time and the precise medical knowledge required by the Healer. Since the spell was guided through the body,

117

understanding which tendons stitched to which bone, which layer of skin—if you even knew about layers of skin! —went where and the like was important. A subset skill within the **Treat** spells even allowed for minor cosmetic improvements. That, Daniel was not intending to learn, but the lower Mana cost was certainly useful.

If he could get the spell to cast.

Cursing under his breath, Daniel felt the Mana forms unravel within the Adventurer's body once more. The hiss under the man's arm, slender and scarred, informed Daniel that his failure had not gone unnoticed. Flashing the man a quick consoling smile, Daniel exhaled and focused again, ignoring the glare sent his way.

Fixing them was a necessity and because of his **Healing Aura**, he was running out of time. Still, haste made waste—in Mana and pain, if nothing else. He would learn this spell, he would learn the physical form and he would not let the damn Master Healer get to him.

***

Trouble arrived the next day in the form of the prince stalking forward, anger warring with disappointment as he joined the team at the Dungeon entrance. Arms crossed, he glared at the group while the Royal Guards stood a short, careful distance behind and watched for potential problems. None of which were arriving, not with their presence being so notable and upfront.

"I heard you all were involved in a bar fight when I left," Roland said accusingly.

"My apologies, your highness. We did attempt to avert the fight," Lady Nyssa said, stepping in smoothly and dropping into a curtsy. It looked strange to Daniel, what with her not wearing a dress, but she certainly played contrite well.

"Brawl," Omrak corrected her.

"What?" Lady Nyssa said, echoed by Roland.

"It's a bar brawl. A fight would entail death. A brawl is done in good fun," Omrak said.

"That . . ." Lady Nyssa paused, then added reluctantly. "I have never known the etymology of such conflicts. I stand corrected."

"It's okay," Omrak said. "You correct me all the time too."

"So, you started a bar *brawl* without me," Roland said. "Causing significant damage and injuring a group of Adventurers."

"Which I have healed," Daniel was quick to point out.

"And you didn't even let me join!" Roland said.

"Wanted join?" Asin said, curiosity making her speak.

"Of course! I've never been in a bar *brawl* before," the prince replied. "Why wouldn't I want to join in such a situation?"

"Because it hurts?" Daniel said.

"It's pointless?" Johan added, speaking up. "You, um, don't even get experience."

"Expensive," was Asin's answer.

"Bah! You don't do such things for the experience points. It's for fun! What's the point of doing all this if not for fun?" Roland replied, snorting at Johan. "Come, Lord Cleese. Surely you know that you will eventually have to give up your sword for more sedate affairs."

"I'm . . . ummm . . . a third son. I don't have an inheritance to . . . uh . . . inherit," Johan said. "Mother says I need to . . . uhh . . . win it."

"So am I! But I still have duties," Roland said. "Anyway, you never know what might happen."

Johan could only shrug, choosing not to contradict the over-eager prince. Lady Nyssa however was quick to cut in. "Prince Roland, I think you misunderstand how common deaths among the noble heirs are. Or even, among royalty."

Roland rolled his eyes. "We've had over a dozen assassinations in my family."

"But none in the last century. Not since your grandfather stabilized the nobility," Lady Nyssa said gently. "Brad has reached a period of peace under your grandfather and father's rule."

"Mmm . . ." Roland said, crossing his arms. He opened his mouth to speak further only to be interrupted by the loud clearing of a throat by the lead guard. Roland sighed, put-upon, but chose not to elaborate, though the entire byplay had Daniel eyeing the prince curiously.

Something else was going on, obviously. Potentially something dangerous enough that they were quite insistent in grabbing an Adventurer with a powerful Gift.

Or perhaps he was just being paranoid.

"Your highness, we shall try to start our next bar brawl when you are around," Omrak said, only to receive a smack off the top of his head by Charles, the only one of them who was tall enough that doing that was an easy action. "Ouch!"

"We are not starting any further *brawls* when my lady or his royal highness are nearby," Charles said, his voice cold. "We do not put our charges into danger, just for fun. If you so desire, I can introduce you to a class of individuals—or a Class even—who would be interested in such pursuits."

"Ooooh . . ." Johan hissed at the burn.

Daniel shook his head at the entire group and, seeing the way the guards and the rest of the Adventurers around them was eyeing the group, clapped his hands together. "All right, enough. We're here to delve, not talk about fights. Some of us have got a bar brawl to pay off."

Grumbling, the team fell into line and Daniel pushed them towards the Dungeon entrance. He was mostly kidding about paying for the brawl—the cost of furniture, while exorbitant to him in some ways, was not much when compared to an Adventurer's take. It was still, however, more than he wanted to pay.

Anyway, if they kept talking about setting up fights or bar brawls, those Royal Guards might just tell on them to the king. And that was one meeting he would be happy to avoid.

Chapter 8

"Do I have to?" Daniel whined, peeking out of the carriage window, fingers spread to push aside the curtain that blocked the view. Fingers brushed against the murky glass, the sensation of touching its coldness muted under the leather gloves he wore.

"The royal family summoned you to the ball. So, yes." Guildmaster Ronson's voice was cold and brooked no argument.

"Requested," Asin pointed out.

"It's the same thing with a royal request," Ronson snapped, rubbing at his long mustaches. "Though you hadn't needed to come. You know it's just going to annoy them."

Asin grinned, flashing all-too-sharp teeth in answer. Ronson rolled his eyes a little, understanding that she was choosing to come, dressed up to the nines as she was in a blousy shirt, tight leather pants, and leather vest combination to tweak the noble's noses.

"At least Omrak chose to avoid it," Ronson said with a sigh to himself. "Though, where was he going?"

"Out with my manservant to get into trouble," Lady Nyssa said, with a roll of her eyes.

"I had not realized he had such . . . lowborn . . . tendencies."

"The things we learn, after multiple years of working for another . . . no?" Ronson said, turning his head to the last member of the carriage. The entire group was a little squished in, what with the carriage meant to carry four and there being five of them.

"Just because you have an unreasonable hatred for zucchinis does not make it a betrayal that I like them," Lady Marshall said.

"Slimy, disgusting . . ." Ronson muttered.

Ignoring the pair, Daniel kept an eye on the outside where the summer twilight hours extended the shadows of the statues and shrubbery of the royal palace while guards patrolled the grounds and carriages sat in line, rolling forward slowly as each new guest was presented.

"I could walk there faster . . ." Daniel muttered, his hand twitching towards the door.

"Touch it, and I'll book another dozen appointments with Lady Suresh," Lady Marshall said warningly.

Daniel visibly shuddered at the mention, unable to stop the automatic reaction. It made Lady Nyssa raise an elegant eyebrow, herself clad in a full court dress in pale cream with a green fronting.

"Oh? Is that the mother or the daughter?" she said, all too lightly.

"Mother," Lady Marshall said, wickedly. "It seems, ever since the death of her husband, she's been . . . active."

"And handsy," Daniel muttered.

"Oh, but she is quite pretty still, like her daughter. Is she not to your liking, Daniel?" Lady Nyssa said, archly.

"Do you know what I—" Daniel clamped his mouth shut, then shook his head. Eventually, he changed what he was going to say slightly. "I'm her Healer. And even if I'm not certified, there are still codes of conduct."

"Mmmmhmmm," Lady Nyssa said, tapping herself on the lips with a fan as she considered Daniel.

"Enough. There's something else I wanted to speak with you all about," Ronson said, cutting them off. "Something you should all be wary of tonight." Those words got the group's attention, as he had intended. "Now, Daniel; you'll obviously be staked out to be tested and flirted with. Try not to fall for any of the young ladies. They'll send you their side family and third or fourth daughters, but no matter how pretty they are, it's not worth getting involved."

Daniel could only nod. Roland had actually taken him aside to mutter the same thing to him when he had passed the invitation, a warning about the ball and what it might entail. It had made Daniel a little more disposed to like the prince. Even if he hated the idea of the actual ball itself.

"More importantly, do not to commit yourself to any additional healing sessions. Those go through the Guild, as you know. Do it once and they'll keep coming and you don't want that." Again, another firm nod. Managing direct approaches was going to be a true headache, one that Daniel had no desire to handle.

"As for you, Asin, your dangers are twofold. There will be tests for your loyalty to the crown, and tests to see if you will join some of the more progressive factions. Try not to engage," Ronson said. "Especially those who try to antagonize you into a physical altercation."

Asin nodded firmly, then pointed with a finger and added. "Food."

Ronson frowned, puzzled, and the Catkin rolled her eyes before yowling and hissing at Daniel. He listened for a bit before he nodded and turned to Ronson.

"She's saying—"

"That she is just going to raid the food. I understand," Ronson cut Daniel off. "That's fine. Just stay out of trouble." Finally, the guildmaster turned to Lady Nyssa, who sat there demurely and patiently. He opened his mouth to say something then shut it, shaking his head.

Relaxing, a little victorious smile flickered at the edges of the noblewoman's lips, even as Lady Marshall gave the younger lady a nod. Then, there was no more time for talking, for it was their turn to alight and be announced. Carriage doors were pulled open, hands were stretched within, and Daniel, bracing himself mentally, readied himself for a truly boring evening.

***

"I'm certain, my lord. You should speak with a real Healer about that kind of boil . . . it's not something I have much experience with," Daniel said, straining to smile at the portly, middle-aged nobleman that had cornered him.

Half an hour into the evening, cornered in one of the many rooms off to the side of the main ball area, Daniel was stuck in conversation with one of the many noblemen who had come to introduce themselves to him. And get a free consult.

"Are you sure? I could show you—"

"I'm certain," Daniel said, adding a little of the authoritative Healer voice he had learnt while working in the hospice.

"Well, all right, then. Just that those Healers are so expensive . . ."

Daniel bit his lip as the older man moved away, the young lady by his side—his third mistress if Daniel recalled correctly—led him away, bedecked in enough jewels that he could have paid for a dozen Healers full-time for a month.

Then again, nobles were all kinds of copper pinchers at times over the strangest things.

***

"You should invest more into your Adventurer Teams, Jospeh." Lord Alric was holding forth, using a wine glass as a prop as he swung it around, threatening to spill the wine over as he punctuated each word. "Beginner Adventurers are hardly worth your time. The real money is to be made in Advanced Adventurers. And if they ever make it to Master…!" A greedy grin flashed across the curly haired, long limbed older man's face.

"Not all of us have Advanced Dungeons to work with. Hosting and paying for them to work the kingdom's dungeons cut down profits significantly," the aforementioned Joseph said, fingers drumming against silk-lined, brown-and-gold trousers. "So long as the kingdom keeps the majority of those Dungeons in their hands, those of us with only a few Beginner Dungeons cannot make the kind of profits you allude to."

"Better to have kingdom Dungeons and have the Adventurers clear them than pay taxes for a standing army like the Albans," Lord Alric said. "Anyway, we have to let our lesser cousins work too, don't you think so, Lady Nyssa?"

The noblewoman, in conversation with another pair of noble ladies a short distance away turned to Lord Alric, arching an eyebrow in query at hearing her name. Daniel snorted, himself overhearing the loud conversation while he—thankfully—had a few moments alone to stuff his face nearby.

"We need Adventurer Guild, kingdom-run Dungeons, don't we? For those who cannot afford to care for such Dungeons themselves?" Lord Alric said.

"The Adventurer Guild does do a good job of ensuring Dungeon outbreaks do not occur," Lady Nyssa said carefully, her eyes flicking over the group as she assessed where this conversation was going and had gone. Daniel knew the kind of assessment she was doing; after all, she was the one who taught him how to gauge political threats.

"A barely adequate job. The funds and resources coming from Dungeons could be more properly managed in the right hands. Rather than a single bureaucratic organization handling everything, we should have local powers overseeing the exploitation of such resources," Joseph said, his fingers never stopping its drumming on his pants.

Lady Nyssa's eyes narrowed, pegging the man for what he was. Another supporter for the newer, richer noble classes, unlike her own. They were the new nobles, many who had bought their way into power, who had abandoned the traditional role of Adventuring as part of their duties but instead wielded land and money.

A brief hesitation, then she smiled at Joseph, Daniel only belatedly realizing he was a member of House Tarth.

"I do believe that the Adventuring Guild offers more than just bureaucracy. Their ability to quickly allocate high-Level Adventurers to deal with Dungeon Breaks and the like are important. We wouldn't want another Ramoutar incident, now would we?" Lady Nyssa said with a smile.

Her thinly veiled barb, recalling a Dungeon break from a noble-controlled Advanced Dungeon, had Joseph glaring back. Before Daniel could continue to listen to the conversation, a smiling servant interposed himself, a card and invitation in hand.

Groaning, Daniel deposited his plate with the man and set off. Another introduction.

***

She was pretty, Daniel had to admit. And the gardens were a nice touch, even if the night was a little chilly, as evidenced by her too-thin gown. Or perhaps that was the point. Still, even if he hadn't been warned beforehand, Daniel would have turned her down. Shaking his head, watching the young girl—barely fifteen if he had to guess—being led off by her chaperone, he stretched a little in the quiet of the gardens. He absently noted the hovering servant a short distance away, the man bearing another invitation.

A few moments of quiet before the servant stepped up, and he was led to another location. One in sight of the resting group of dancers on the balcony, but far enough away that anyone without a Skill Proficiency would not be able to hear them.

Where another lady waited. This one older, though slim and matronly.

"Healer Daniel," she greeted him, a hand outstretched.

"Duchess Zovag, a pleasure," Daniel said as he took her hand, bowing over it and then releasing it. "And it's just Adventurer. I do not have the Healing Guild's certification."

"A matter of time, I say." The Duchess smiled. "A handsome and Gifted boy like you, they'd be fools to give that up. Even if some people are too jealous to see it." A glance to the side, where Rotfield stood, swanning around with others.

"Thank you for your kind words," Daniel said, choosing not to say anything further.

"Not at all. Now, I understand you are single?" Daniel blinked, surprised at how direct she was. The duchess grinned saucily, before leaning in. A part of Daniel winced, bracing for flirting before she continued. "Tell me, would you like to meet my son?"

"Your son?" Daniel said, surprised.

"Yes, I heard you've been turning the young ladies down left and right so I assumed—"

"No!" Daniel shook his head. "I'm not . . . not that there's anything wrong with that but . . ."

"Oh. A pity." The duchess sighed and leaned back, then suddenly eyed Daniel up and down. "You know, I'm single too—"

"Asin. My friend." Daniel said, struggling.

"You're into Beastkin?"

"No, she needs my help. I'm sorry, I need to go." Daniel gulped and moved, hurrying off.

What was it with these older noble women being so forward?

***

"Tell me, Adventurer Chai, what do you think of the prince and his antics with your team? Surely, real Adventurers do not want to be bothered by those playing at danger?" A smiling nobleman, white haired and with a cane, wearing a brocade of green and gold, stood before him. Even if he smiled a lot, Daniel could tell, there wasn't much warmth in it at all.

That the man had waved him over, almost sending his little toadies to drag him into the conversation that he was having with a half-dozen other older men spoke to his plans. And now, all of them were watching Daniel, looking for him to say something.

Weighing him.

So he smiled, bowed. Spoke the truth, because he knew Skills were in play. The Guildmaster had said as much. "Prince Roland has learnt to fit into our team quite well. And no one who actually dares the Dungeons is playing at danger. It's very real and present, and all of us, whether royalty or commoner, attempt to reduce it."

"Still, it's not as though he's in real danger, what with all his bodyguards," the smiling nobleman drawled, making Daniel's teeth stand on edge. But he saw the trap there, though he wondered the point. Anyone paying attention would know this.

"There are no bodyguards, not in the Dungeon," Daniel said, going for the truth. He could lie or attempt to obfuscate, but what was the point? It's not as though the bodyguards outside the Dungeon entrance were hard to miss.

"So, a royal heir risks his life—a life much more important than any commoners—playing at Adventurer."

Another voice, wheezy and grumpy. The speaker was old, like the original, a nobleman of some lineage that Daniel could not place. No major House then. He still hadn't learnt all the minor Houses and their colors, but he could place the initial speaker as a noble from the House of Zaynastra one of those opposing the royal family.

Still, Daniel could at least be grateful he gave him an out. "Well, my lord, this commoner thinks all lives are equally important." A sketched bow, and then Daniel stepped back, keeping his body ramrod straight. He was not as angry or insulted as he made it seem. He knew how some of these nobles thought.

But it gave him a chance to escape.

Even if he felt he'd lost out in that conversation in some ephemeral way.

***

In the corner, Asin was hunkering down over her plate, a crab leg in one hand and held as though she was using it to ward off the trio of men standing around her. The Catkin's ears were laid flat against her head, her tail stiff behind her body and guarded. As Daniel neared, he managed to overhear them speak.

"Is the food good then? I bet your kind never get to try such tasty work . . . best eat up. You never know when it'd be your last meal," the floppy-haired, center-parted blond taunted Asin, his minions chuckling along.

Daniel growled a little, watching the trio at work, but Asin had a perfect rejoinder. Rather than speak, she raised the crab leg and bit into it, sharp teeth piercing the shell and cracking it. The noise and her subsequent chewing disgusted the trio, who all flinched, even as Asin kept eye contact with the blond in front.

"Barbaric beast!"

Crunch!

"You . . ."

Crack!

"Excuse me . . ." Daniel cleared his throat, catching the blond as he raised his hand, frustration turning to physical dissuasion. Rather than let that carry on, the Healer chose to act. "I'm sure the king and his family would prefer there be no blood be shed. Even if I can heal it."

The trio spun around, the blond's eyes narrowing. He raised his chin unconsciously, staring down at Daniel pass his nose. "Ah, the commoner Healer. Of course you're here defending your pet."

"Not her. You," Daniel said. "You forget, we're Adventurers. Taking apart effete nobles who are twenty pounds too heavy and likely haven't seen the inside of a sparring yard in a decade would be easier than killing kobolds.

"And we've killed a lot of kobolds."

"You dare!"

Daniel grinned and stepped closer, meeting the man's eyes as he neared. Then, he turned slowly, making the other turn a little too till they both caught sight of the pair of discreet royal guards standing, watching the altercation.

"I dare."

Fuming, the floppy-haired nobleman stepped back. "Whatever. Ride your favor. When you fall out, know that we'll be waiting."

"Sure . . . and we'll be right here. By the crab legs!" Daniel said, waving goodbye to the trio.

Asin, having watched the interaction snorted a little, the huff of air escaping her scrunched nose. Then, when Daniel had stepped closer, snagging a crab leg from her plate, she added, "Bad."

"Yes, sorry. I probably shouldn't have."

A nod, then Asin turned her head. To Daniel's lack of surprise, the pair of guards hovering had come closer to the pair.

"The king would like to speak with you, Healer."

"Of course." Daniel dropped the crab leg aside, wiped his hands on a courtesy napkin, and gestured for the guards to lead the way.

***

"Adventurer Chai, Rotfield complains that you do not take full advantage of the time you have with him," the king announced, the moment Daniel had finished his greetings.

"I apologize, my liege. I do my best but . . ."

"You have Adventuring with my son and these healing sessions with other nobles to do, no?" The king shook his head, fingers drumming against his pants. The pair were standing in a secluded balcony overlooking the main dance hall below, their conversation and occupancy of the alcove. shrouded by enchantments.

"Yes, my liege."

"Well, Adventuring and healing has always been a complex interaction," the king said, rubbing his chin. "Best get used to balancing things better. I dislike having my Royal Healer complain to me every day during our checkup."

"Yes, my liege. I shall strive to do better."

141

"Good." A pause. "How is my son doing?"

Daniel hesitated, curious to know if this question was asked from a father's perspective or a king's. Then, realizing he really had no clue how he would adjust his answer anyway, Daniel chose to tell the truth. "He is adjusting to working with my team. We have hope to clear the Advanced Dungeon soon."

"Will you be racing then, to complete it?"

Daniel nodded.

"Good. Roland was always a little too independent and enthusiastic. Being forced to work with others should help," the king mused. Then, turning to Daniel, he continued. "You understand that this time with my son is temporary? At the very least, he will be married to another to strengthen the nation. At the worst . . ."

At the worst, he would be needed as a replacement heir or heir itself. In either case, being an Adventurer and delving would be barred. Even if leading armies were not that much safer, it was more socially acceptable.

"Yes, my liege. And I will guard him while I can."

"Good." Turning away, the king flipped a hand to dismiss Daniel, who gladly scurried out, only then realizing how much of a cold sweat he had gained. Meeting the king was always a little nerve-wracking, especially for a commoner like him.

But with his duties done, Daniel was free to enjoy the ball. As much as one could even as another young lady floated over, a smile on her face, the matron who was in charge of watching her right behind, glaring at Daniel disapprovingly.

Definitely as much as he could.

Chapter 9

"This is an unacceptable risk," the lead Royal Guardsman growled, mustache quivering like a rodent had made its residence on his lips. He was standing close to Prince Roland as he spoke, his voice low but not so low that Daniel could not hear it. "Your highness."

"Oh, it'll be fine," Roland said, clapping the guard on the shoulder. "It's not as though I'm going alone. And multiple teams go in every month."

"Multiple experienced teams," the guardsman ground out. "Teams who stand a chance at completing the Dungeon and who have the Skills to map the new labyrinth."

"But we have that. Daniel has a Mapping Skill, and I've got the Labyrinth Orb," Roland said patiently. "And we nearly completed the Dungeon last month!"

"Nearly is not done," the guardsman said, exasperated.

"It's fine. We won't go farther than a few turns. We're not actually trying to get to the center," Roland replied. "We just want to help with the mapping."

"Just because you don't intend to try doesn't mean you won't stumble on it!" the guardsman snapped.

"And if we do, we'll finish it." Roland smiled. His eyes grew somber, while he added, "You forget, I do have ways of finishing this if necessary."

The Royal Guardsman tensed but relaxed a little, though the way he looked around and shot Daniel and Asin, the two companions close enough to hear—in the Beastkin's case, due to her innate better hearing—a suspicious glare. But, after a moment, he stepped back, giving a close-fisted salute.

"Your highness. Good delving."

Grinning insouciantly, Roland waved to the guards and sauntered over to the rest of the group. As Daniel turned, he caught one last meaningful glare sent his way by the leading guardsman and winced. He knew what it meant, being the Healer and team leader.

And what kind of responsibility that was.

A shake of his head sent such erroneous thoughts aside as Daniel met with the group. Theirs was not the only one gathered at the

Dungeon entrance early in the morning, the courtyard leading to it lit with the steady glow of Mana lamps, what with the fall sun not having risen. Plumes of warm breath, visible in the cold rose from nearby mouths as the Adventurers stared at one another, the teams looking to explore the newly reconfigured Dungeon waiting by one another. Occasionally, the more gregarious broke off to chat with other team members, but with the opening so close, most chose to stay close.

Not that Daniel saw a huge point to that. The Adventuring Guild would be streaming them in order of seniority, which meant for themselves, they would be waiting quite a while. He could, he assumed probably have pulled rank with the prince but to the prince's credit, he had never even mentioned that. Neither would Daniel even consider doing that.

After all, with the way the Labyrinth dumped them into random locations, the advantage of going first was not as great as newcomers might expect. Nor was Daniel inclined to make use of such advantages. He shuddered to even think the kind of rumors it would create.

Caught up in his own thoughts, he was broken out of it by a meat pastry waved in front of his face, the concentrated smell of heavy spices waking him. Blinking, Daniel took the pastry from the furred hand, offering a return grin to his friend. Then, remembering his own duties, he called out to the group.

"Best eat up now. We won't be stopping once we're in."

***

Labyrinth ruins and slug creatures. Daniel grunted as he raised the crossbow he had stored for such instances, firing the enchanted bolt forwards to strike his target off the ceiling. The bolt only penetrated an inch into the slimy muscle before it stopped, but it was enough. The cold enchantment took over, wrapping the creature in ice magic and forcing it to curl inwards. Losing grip of the ceiling, it fell downward to crack, its frozen body taking further damage.

"Going in!" Johan cried, darting around Omrak.

The big Northerner halted his swing for a second; the ruined wall that had given way to create an earth embankment, the place he had chosen to take a stand, gave him the best position to hold the monsters off.

Not that it mattered to Johan. Wielding a pair of swords that flickered into flames, his **Elemental Blade** Skill allowing him to wield whatever elemental attack he wished, he tore into the Iskma Slugs. Not that Daniel knew who or what Iskma was, but he had obviously named the disgusting creatures.

So disgusting that Asin, who normally was happy to take part in any fight, was standing well behind the lines, throwing her knives whenever they reappeared and shocking the monsters off their perches on the wall and ceilings.

"You should save your bolts," Lady Nyssa murmured to Daniel from where she stood next to him, hands held by her side. She did not cast anything, seeing little point.

They were only two turns in, and these creatures were just explode-y and gooey, with a minor acidic burn to them. If they managed to clamp on to you with their multi-lined teeth, it might go badly, but they were slow and dumb.

Not a threat for a team like them.

"Yeah." Daniel nodded and slipped the bolt back into his **Inventory.** In the meantime, his eyes tracked over to the prince who, unlike Johan, had chosen to stay in his position just to the left of Omrak. Guarding the Northerner's back but not interfering with his swings.

As though he was acknowledging this, Omrak flicked his greatsword one last time and then stepped back.

"Your turn!" Omrak cried.

Grinning, the prince burst forward, sword swinging and shield held before him. Daniel knew that the Royal Bodyguards would have quailed at such risk—low as it might be—but that was the reason Roland was with them. To have a chance to put himself in peril, to test himself without the stuffy eyes of his guards.

Holding the line was simple enough, though it was a messy business. Blade slipping forwards and sideways, Roland kept to quick cuts and thrusts, tearing open delicate skin and hiding behind his shield whenever the bodies before him burst apart in retaliation. His shield and armor, the best of its kind, was more than adequate for dealing with such pitiful-Leveled creatures.

After a while, the number of slug creatures had dropped that Daniel called out to Roland. "Advance!"

Released at last, Roland bounded forward, his sword dipping left and right as it skewered and killed. Igniting the enchantment within the weapon itself, Roland tore into the monsters with renewed vengeance in an attempt to match Johan's own slaughter.

It was, of course, a failure since Johan had significant advantages including the use of two weapons and a head start. Still, it did nothing to stop Roland and Omrak who came along soon after in joining the battle. In all too short a period, all that was left were the glittering shards of Mana stones, the core of the creatures that Erlis used to create them from Ba'al's taint.

Reward and necessity, all in one package.

Breathing heavily, Roland stood beside Johan, patting the man on the shoulder with one free hand, a wide grin on his face. "Master of Arms for sure. In a decade, I'm sure you'll be a true Weaponmaster. At that time, I expect you to be training my own household guard."

"Your highness . . ." Johan blushed, head bowing in embarrassment.

By his side, Daniel noted how Lady Nyssa stiffened for a second before breaking into a genuine grin at the boy's fortune. Daniel understood; the kind of patronage just casually offered to the young man was more than sufficient to set him up for life. Him and his extended family, an aspect that Daniel knew would make his overbearing mother happy.

Everything that a noble could want. Everything that Lady Nyssa wanted, for herself, for her family. And she smiled, to see someone else get it.

Then, that moment was over, and it was just a team, getting sorted for the next fight.

***

"Behind!" Charles roared, the group trapped in the narrow tunnel, monsters coming down one side and the other. Tall, monstrous, empty armors, as much empty spirits as creatures of physical reality. Each were nine feet tall, wielding massive weapons that shook the melee fighters when blocked or pushed aside. The five at the front had already hampered their advance, and now, three more arrived from behind.

Daniel spun around, his eyes flicking over options. He ran the numbers, made the decision and gestured at Asin, who had been hanging back, searching for an opening in the front, and who had now turned around.

"Hold. Take the front down, then come to us," Daniel commanded.

Her eyes narrowed, but then she nodded and turned back. He could feel her bounce on her light, padded feet, a slight sheen crossing over her skin and fur. He knew she'd just activated another ability, **Cat's Grace**, a Beastkin skill that boosted her speed and grace. The next second, even as he was turning away to the back, to where their Mage was already facing, forming a **Sonic Ball** in her hand, he caught her darting away. As graceful as a cat.

Then, he had no more time to consider his back. "Hit them hard."

"I'll need a few seconds," Lady Nyssa said.

Daniel nodded, having already guessed as much. He moved forward, stopping a short distance from where he started, positioning himself just in front and to the side of Charles. The bodyguard had put away his bow, drawing forth a smaller shield and a mace from his inventory.

At Daniel's questioning look, Charles shrugged. "Just because I prefer the sword doesn't mean I wasn't trained with maces."

Then, the pair no longer had time to talk. The empty Spirit Armors might be slow moving, but they were so large, they still covered the ground to the party fast enough. With all three of their main melee combatants already caught up in the skirmish against the armors to the front—a mistake Daniel was kicking himself at making now—it was up to the Healer and Charles to hold them back.

Good thing, Daniel thought as he hefted his shield, he was trained for this too. His first action was to split the group apart. That was easily done by casting his **Impactful Hammer of Recall** forwards, sending it to strike the monster on the far right in the chest. The creature flew backwards, the **Impactful** enchantment on the warhammer boosting the kinetic punch delivered.

Next, Daniel grabbed his old warhammer from his reserve, pulling on its enchantment. The Monstrous Spider that emerged was not the most appropriate creature to use in this fight, but it was what was stored in the hammer's summoning rune. For now, it would work.

A step backwards, allowing Charles to cover for him as he stored his additional weapon. The bodyguard flickered as he moved to meet the lead armor, his shield held before him. **Intercepting Charge** allowed the bodyguard to move into the blow with surprising speed, blasting the armor backwards as his own **Shield of Rebound** took care of the strike. It moved the armor back by a few feet, more than enough for Charles to begin to lay into it with his own, unenchanted weapon.

In the meantime, Daniel held his hand out, recalling his weapon to him as he skipped left, taking on the last monster. It raised its arm high overhead, ready to swing its oversized sword down. Rather than let the monster finish its swing, Daniel charged in and caught the elbow of its armor on his raised shield, pushing with all his considerable strength. As he did so, he stepped to the side, swinging hard with his own weapon, the hammer finally landing in his outstretched hand.

Strike. And strike again. The hammer he used crushed steel in degrees over the strikes Daniel himself threw. Each strike drained the kinetic reservoir, but as the pair traded blow, that very same kinetic reserve grew. Increasing with every swing, every block that did not strike hammer head, where the enchantment would trigger.

Long moments of battering one another occurred, one that Daniel found himself mostly on the receiving end. Even damaging the externalities of the creature's body did nothing to the animating presence within. Only by cracking the armor open entirely would the Spirits within be forced outwards, losing cohesion outside of its protective embrace.

A task that required great strength or great finesse. Neither of which the Healer had. Breathing grew hard, his arms ached with repeated blows, his own armor-shedding attacks that still left him bruised underneath it all. His legs wavered, his arms throbbed, and the third monster returned, having dispatched the monstrous summoned spider with ease, forcing Daniel and Charles to stand in line, fighting off the creatures.

"Ready!"

The shout came none too soon. Ducking low, the pair hunkered down even as the screaming orb of sound and fury passed over their heads. It even crossed through the top of an armor's helmet, sending the creature twisting and sprawling to the ground as the animating Spirit twitched in agony. The other pair of armors soon followed their brethren, the sonic attack bypassing steel shells.

Long seconds of thrumming damage, before Daniel shoved Charles in the side and gestured with his head. Together, the pair braved the screaming aural attack to pound upon the armors, cracking them open to hasten the monsters' death.

Leaving them, long minutes later, victorious.

If rather bruised and exhausted.

***

The team reconvened after a few minutes of rest and preparation, weapons stored away, wounds bandaged and discarded weapons—in Johan's case mostly, though Asin's throwing knives were also at fault—picked up. Asin had even retrieved all the Mana stones, helped along by Charles doing a final sweep to ensure nothing was missed. Not that there were likely to be, since they weren't fighting a swarm. Still, it always paid to be careful—literally. More than once, the team had picked up Mana stones left behind by other, less careful teams.

Daniel swept over the group, then decided to just ask rather than gingerly move around it. "Resources?"

"About half of my Mana pool," Lady Nyssa said.

"Two-thirds," Daniel said, glancing over the team. No one was hurt, hurt—but pushing a few Healer Mark's at the end of the day to ensure everyone was ready for the next day would cost him at least a third of his Mana. His **Healing Aura** might accelerate base healing, but it just wasn't that powerful.

Yet.

"I'm down to a quarter," Johan spoke up, looking down and shifting uncomfortably. "Had to . . . ummm . . . use a Skill."

"The one that punched through the armor?" Omrak rumbled. "Beautiful attack. What was it? **Piercing Strike**?"

"Uhh . . . no. It was . . . ummm . . . Masters of Arms exclusive."

"Of course! And . . . ?" Omrak persisted.

"Friend Omrak, you know that is rude," Roland cut in, nodding to Johan. "Suffice to say, our Master of Arms has a powerful piercing skill proficiency, no?"

Omrak jerked a nod, pounding his chest with a fist. "I am good to continue."

"As am I," Roland agreed. When the group just stared at him, he looked back with a knowing smile. "Really. My armor refreshes my Stamina, and I took the least amount of injury."

"Omrak and Roland are good. Charles?" Daniel said, turning to the older gentleman. He was watching their back as usual, standing just outside.

"I have three quarters of my Mana left."

"Two thirds." Asin spoke up, before she was asked.

Daniel paused, considering as he swept his gaze over the team, assessing damage and stamina. Mostly, it was good, the **Healing Aura** helping his friends recover their endurance faster than anything else. However, their biggest damage dealers were low on Mana which meant they would struggle against another high-level team. If they ran into a couple more such groups, returning would be tricky.

Even so, a quick mental gauge and review of their map showed that they'd only been in the Dungeon for less than half a day and were only just over two dozen turns in. Nowhere close to completing the Dungeon or finding its heart.

More importantly . . . Daniel cast a glance under his brows over to the eager prince, only to be surprised to see the prince smiling back a little. Before the Healer could consider what that meant, the prince spoke up.

"Let's head back," Roland said. "We don't want my guards to worry too much. Better to be safe than sorry, right?"

The group nodded automatically, both because Roland was telling the truth and because it was the prince speaking. Even then, Daniel was surprised to hear the words coming from the impetuous prince's mouth.

Then he shook it off and gestured.

"Well, then, let's go. Asin?"

Nodding, the Catkin loped off, taking the lead as they backtracked. If they were lucky, none of the monsters had respawned and leaving would be simple. If they were even luckier, some wandering monsters might have arrived and they'd be able to pick up a few more Mana stones.

Chapter 10

After their initial push to test themselves in the new, reconfigured Dungeon, the team returned again and again. Within months, they became a contender in the race to clear the Dungeon first. By unspoken agreement, such contests were something that the Master Class or higher teams left to the Advanced Adventurers, passing on the same benefits and competition levels they themselves had experienced. The grindstone of competition both aided the teams in developing while ensuring that the more important Master Class Dungeon was well provisioned with members.

On occasion, the team would even enter Warmount, the aforementioned Master Class Dungeon. Always without their royal member though, for they had been firmly informed doing so would not be allowed. While there were numerous quests and locations within the sprawling Dungeon itself that could benefit even Advanced Adventurers like them, there was always a risk—miniscule perhaps, but a risk—of a breakthrough or powerful, Master Class monsters.

Outside of the Dungeon runs, the team found themselves more and more socially connected. Classes on etiquette gave way to practical exercises, dinners and lunches, soirees and balls at noble estates. More than once, the team—and guild, who managed their time— were offered exclusive quests. Any that required travel were turned down by the team, other members of the guild dispatched.

Those local might see the team's presence. Soon enough, the society of nobles had come to an understanding of the group's modus operandi, taking only legitimate jobs that tested their prowess and skills and which paid well. Threadbare excuses to spend time with the prince were discarded aside, often picked up by other members of the Seven Stones guild.

Even then, the team had more than enough such assignments. Whether it was the cleansing of an monster-swarmed river or a hunt for a new alpha predator in the grounds surrounding the city, the numerous sprawling lands that the nobles had claimed and, ostensibly, guarded had to be cleansed of threats. It was part of the social contract, to ensure that the king's own men did not trample within.

Months passed in short order, one season turning to the next. By the time winter arrived, the team was well organized, the flood of fall adventuring quests outside the dungeon giving way to that awkward period when winter had not arrived in the deepest depths, leaving the most dangerous monsters outside. Instead, the changing of the seasons brought even more dreaded things.

Balls and further soirées.

To those, the team were dragged, forced to interact with greater familiarity if not comfort. Rumblings of the dangerous political games continued, though most members of the party were spared any such direct plays. Their alliances were laid bare; even delicate probes were withdrawn.

In time, even Asin's presence had been accepted, if not agreed upon. The Catkin was more than once forced into uncomfortable social situations, but it was Omrak who caused their first major embarrassment. The lusty young

Northerner was caught in a compromising situation with the wife of a minor nobleman. The resulting scandal and duel—which Omrak handily won against the house guard captain—was the talk of the town for weeks.

Until, of course, the next scandal arose.

In the meantime, the Seven Stones Guild flourished. Guildmaster Ronson and Vice-Guildmistress Lady Marshall made the most of their newfound prestige and inflow of capital via dedicated quests, increasing the number and size of the guild. New buildings—close by to the guild—were purchased, new residences expanded upon. Pressure was applied, political and gold in sufficient quantities to make their long-time neighbor to sell away their land, leading to significant upgrades and expansion of the guild hall.

In many ways, for all the concerns of royalty or guildmaster, the prince's addition had been, if not entirely successful at the beginning, a marvelous result now.

It was all this marvelous fortune that Daniel turned over in his mind, over and over again, as he lay in bed one morning; as winter cold howled outside his cozy residence and wondered:

Why, exactly, was he dissatisfied?

***

The party was gathered at the bottom of the stairs, in the foyer of the expanded guild hall. Everyone was up and ready, eager to begin another day delving. Daniel was the last to make his way down, rubbing the sleep from his eyes and trying to decide if using his Gift to wake him further was a wasteful use of his memories.

"Ah, our Healer has arrived at last. Shall we?" Lady Nyssa said, offering Daniel a smile as he approached the group.

"The Labyrinth again?" Daniel said.

A variety of nods greeted his question. Asin, perhaps knowing Daniel best, tilted her head to the side as she regarded him, her ears swiveling down.

"Let's not," Daniel said impetuously.

"Ah, a request then?" Roland said, rubbing his chin. "We have not done one in a few weeks.

Though, I thought your guildmaster had indicated nothing of . . . appropriate . . . form had arrived. Unless you've changed your mind about Lady Mosej's invitation?" A leering grin.

"No." Daniel shook his head firmly. QuanEr's mercy be upon him, those noblewomen were just relentless. "No request. We're Adventurers, not errand boys. Or . . . stuffed-peacock bodyguards."

A slight stir, from the Royal Guards. Daniel did not care, even if what he had said might be considered an insult to them. He was tired, dissatisfied. He needed a change, something more.

"Let's do Warmount."

His words drew a shocked silence from the group as they stared at him. The truth was, running Warmount with its wider array of assignments and tasks was a common thing about the Adventuring teams in the capital. The team – sans Roland – had done it repeatedly. But it was that – the without the prince – that was the sticking point.

"No." The lead Royal Guard stepped forward, lips thinning as he glared at Daniel. "You may not risk the prince in such a place."

"I'm not risking anything," Daniel said, crossing his arms. "He's choosing to come with us—if he does—entirely on his own accord."

"The agreement with the king—"

"There is no agreement," Daniel said. "Just a promise to keep him alive. Which I will. Or die trying."

"It's not your death we're concerned about."

"Which is all too clear," Daniel groused. "Nor do I care about what you think." Turning away from the man, a man that Daniel knew could easily kill him, he spoke to the third prince. "Will you join us?"

"I . . ." Roland was hesitating, caught by surprise by the shift in plans. His gaze was conflicted. "We, this . . ."

"What he's trying to say is that this is a party decision, not just yours," Lady Nyssa said, touching Daniel on the upper arm till he turned to her fully. "And it's not one that we have discussed."

"What is there to discuss? We go to Warmount all the time," Daniel said. "It offers better coin, better experience, better training. There's more to learn at Warmount than we can ever learn running the Labyrinth. I'm tired of walking twisting corridors every few days."

"We could . . . ummm . . . go to other . . . Dungeons," Johan said, shifting uncomfortably. "There's some . . . in days' journeys."

His words garnered nods from the group, including the Royal Guards. Daniel sniffed. "I bet they'd want to plan the trip weeks in advance. Make sure we had a proper place to stay, double check the inn, maybe even have their people run the Dungeon beforehand."

"Wait," Roland said, looking at Daniel. "Are you tired of me, rather than the Dungeon?"

He sounded hurt, making the Healer regret the way he acted. But . . .

"It's not you. It's all this." A hand rose, waving around him. "I'm tired of being on display. Of not being, well, what I want to be."

"And what is that?" the guard captain asked.

"An Adventurer!"

"You don't think you're one with me around?" Roland said.

"Not a real one."

"Ah . . . and of course, that means I'm not one too . . ." Roland trailed off, nodding. "Of course. I should have known."

He turned away, heading for the door.

"Where are you going?" Lady Nyssa called.

"Home. I find myself out of sorts and unfit for delving today," Roland said.

Lady Nyssa spun around, glaring at Daniel. He just kept his arms crossed, refusing to say anything even as Roland and his men walked out, leaving the group alone.

To everyone's surprise, it was Johan who spoke up next. "Me too." Then, suiting action to words, he walked out, leaving the team down another member.

Leg tapping, Lady Nyssa continued to stare at Daniel till she let out a frustrated huff. "Idiot man-child!"

Throwing her hands up, she stalked out after Johan and Roland, leaving Daniel alone. When he turned to look at the remaining two—Charles following his lady as always—he found no support. In fact, at some point, Asin had slipped away, leaving him to stare at Omrak who just shook his head at Daniel before heading for the dining room where breakfast was still being served.

And then, he was alone.

"Fine! I didn't need you all anyway."

So saying, Daniel walked out of the guild hall to head for the Dungeon. He would still run it, if nothing else. After all, everyone needed a Healer.

***

"The prince is at his studies and will not be having guests today," the palace guard announced to Lady Nyssa, the polearm shifted to block her entrance to the palace grounds. Or technically, the inner palace grounds since she was already in the palace. She'd lost him on the way, not having moved fast enough to follow in his wake and thus forced to actually deal with foot and carriage traffic.

Lady Nyssa's eyes narrowed, then she nodded curtly but politely to the guard. As much as it frustrated her, the guard was just doing his job. There was absolutely no reason to get angry with him. He certainly had no power to gainsay a royal command.

Turning on her heel, she moved with Charles on her heels to leave the palace before something else ruined her day. That damn idiotic Healer, that obtuse, mule-headed, muscular fool who . . .

"Ah, Lady Nyssa. Not Adventuring today?" A voice cut through her mental rant, forcing her to pause and stop by its very presence in front of her.

"Lady Walraus," Lady Nyssa said, turning over and offering a curtsy. She had to, after all she was but the child of a lower noble, compared to Lady Walraus; who was the wife of a viscount. It did not, however, mean that she had to like her or provide a too-warm welcome. They were, after all, on opposite sides of the brewing political battle.

"Oh? No answer? Well, it's not necessary of course. Everyone knows the prince came storming back, all angry and in a snit before locking himself away. Then again, what can you expect? From a *royal*." The words were said almost with a sneer. Almost.

Lady Nyssa looked around and noticed that a few of the other wandering noblemen, pages, and servants had either slowed down or blatantly turned to listen in on this conversation. Her tone, her challenge, it was all very clear that they were attempting another power play.

And it was up to her to squash it.

"Yes. We had a disagreement today," Lady Nyssa said, choosing the best option here. Truth. If the woman knew of the argument already, it was better to work with the truth than to concoct a lie that would be exposed later. It would harm her own position an what she had to say. "Dungeon parties have them, all the time. But you know that, after all, your family has done so much delving." Sickly-sweet tone, so much so because everyone knew the Walraus had not. They were merchants, given status because of their money and not because of any force of

173

arms. A new kind of noble, and one that needed to be nipped in the bud. "When you have a group of highly motivated, highly skilled individuals working together, conflict occurs.

"It's not about the conflict though."

Then Lady Nyssa paused. And waited.

"And what is it about?" Lady Walraus said.

Her family might have been smart at making money, but none of those smarts had passed on to Lady Walraus at all. If not for the fact that she was pretty and had a way with some of the older men on the council, Lady Nyssa was sure she would have been taken out of the capital long ago. Such an obvious trap.

"It's about how we end things." A beat. "And an Adventuring party always ends things well."

Then, a quick curtsy while the woman was trying to work out what she meant, and Lady Nyssa swept away. Mentally, she cursed herself for that last sentence. It could have been worded better. Something with a little more sting, and maybe a hint of a threat. But like the Lady, she was not a political animal herself. She was just an

Adventurer, thrust into the middle of politics she had no right to be within.

"Well done, m'lady." Charles cut into her spiraling thought, having moved ahead to hold open a door. He had led her, without her prompting, down some side corridors so that they could exit the palace via one of the side entrances. Not a servant's entrance, but close to it.

"I could have done better."

"Then you shall practice." Charles paused, then tilted his head backwards, his eyes growing dark and somber. "I fear we will all have more than enough chance."

"All but that idiot."

"Well, yes. The Healer is rather insulated due to his Gift."

Running a hand through her hair, Lady Nyssa turned from side to side, taking in their position. Then, a slight smile crossed her face as she realized where she was. In fact . . .

"Just down the street, there's this lovely tea shop . . ."

"Yes, m'lady," Charles said amiably. He watched as she wandered off and let out a tiny relieved breath of his own as she went to pick up a treat.

As for himself, he could not help but remember the dark looks and the additional presence of men with swords. More bodyguards like himself, more than ever. On both sides. For all the wars of words that were going on right now, the way it cut down and raised up various individuals, those attacks were—beyond the occasional suicide—bloodless.

But old instincts were telling the bodyguard the war that was coming might not stay as bloodless as many hoped for much longer. And, obviously, his was not the only Skill triggering.

Chapter 11

"See? Perfectly peaceful, didn't I tell you?" Daniel said just as he ducked under a swipe of a swinging flail. It passed over his head, brushed against the top of his helmet, its user snarling at the Healer who proceeded to turn his shield on its side. Edge facing the man clambering over the crenelation, Daniel then triggered a **Shield Bash**, punching forwards. Still half-gripping the ladder he had used to clamber upwards, the man flew backwards, pulling ladder and those behind him off the wall of the giant castle.

Daniel couldn't help but grin a little, watching the man fall off the wall and take a bunch of others with him. "Love it when they do that. If you time it just right, they always just grab harder."

"Great, but we don't get their Mana stones that way," Omrak said.

To punctuate his point, he reached over and grabbed his own opponent by the arm, pulling him over the wall and tossing him behind to the grounds below. The main flailed, falling the long thirty feet before he hit the courtyard.

Shouts from within indicated how unhappy those within the courtyard were with Omrak's method of keeping Mana stones within the lobby, a point that Asin would have hissed to her friends. If she thought it would make a difference. And if she was not right then in the middle of leaping off a nearby crenelation to land on a flying harpy, her two knives threading themselves to the soft shoulder joints of the creature's back. The two tumbled downwards, only for the Catkin to leap off the monster with a push of her legs to land, feet first, onto a new assailant to crush him down. A quick spin and stab ended him too.

"I would not call this peaceful," Roland said, standing on the opposite side of the three, backed up by Johan on the other side and a watchful Lady Nyssa and Charles.

The pair were positioned at the top of the tower wall, keeping an eye on the party and launching the occasional attack when necessary. Charles much more often than the Mage of course, since the runners—Beginner Adventurers one and all—kept him amply supplied with arrows.

"They do these wall pushes twice a day at least," Daniel said, standing around and eyeing the group.

He was positioned in the center of the wall with an impromptu healing station set up right behind him. The simple wooden shed that helped stop arrows from raining down on them—not that many could even make the angle—also helped to house the injured, conjured soldiers and Adventurers. As it was, the Adventuring team spread out across the wall were more of a force multiplier to the entire thing, rather than being expected to hold the wall by themselves.

"I know. I do live here, you know," the prince said sarcastically. He shoved forwards with his sword, beheading another clamberer, the human face of their assailant looking surprised for a brief second before shutting down as he fell. "I've heard all the stories."

"Stories aren't reality," Daniel replied.

"But this seems close enough." Looking around, Roland nodded and raised his sword hand. It glowed for a second, filling with light and he stepped up to the wall's edge. A quick swing down of his sword cut at the various individuals below, the shining light arcing outwards.

"What was that?" Daniel said, his surprise allowing one of the attackers to strike at him. He growled and bashed the poor fighter over the arm a couple of times before the mixed human-and-Beastkin Dungeon spawn fell off the side of the building, all the while his side smarting. Thankfully, his plate armor had taken the majority of the attack, but the energy transferred still hurt.

"**Royal Cut**," Roland said, leaning on his sword a little with its point dug into the ground. A couple of other Adventurers were side-eyeing the prince for his casual use of a Legendary weapon as a prop, but no one said anything. Among other things, the weapon wasn't likely to lose any durability over such a small thing.

"Never saw you use it before," Daniel said.

For a moment, the group had a bit of a break and so they took the time to drink water, wrap wounds and rest while the NPCs took care of the fighting. Not that there was much going on, not with the prince's latest attack taking out the line of ladders along the area they guarded.

"It's not as useful in the Labyrinth," Roland said. "It works off the number of individuals within close proximity and within my Aura." He nodded to the various NPCs working the walls and added, "They count."

"Oh, one of those Skills." Daniel nodded.

He knew of them. It was how Nobles and the Royalty managed to keep their position at times, because Skills that allowed them to pull upon the greater populace gave them an advantage in some ways over plain commoners like him. It wasn't foolproof of course, but it did make having a prince on the battlefield—like the First Prince—an important factor in engagements. Of course, it also meant that things like assassins and poisoners were important, which was why Healers like himself were so vital.

And what a revelation it was for the poor Adventurer, to understand the intricate checks and balances that kept everything running at a higher level. Push things out of whack too far— like, for example, a Gifted Healer who could handle any poison or injury if given time—and you suddenly caused the entire edifice to become unstable. For Nobles kept the Royalty in check, while the threat of massed uprisings and, yes, Adventurers leading them kept both Nobles and Royalty watching one another.

A deep rumbling, one that Daniel had been hearing for a while but now seemed much more pertinent, drew his attention back to the present. By the side, one of the Master Class teams was waving for their team even as another pair of Beginner Adventuring teams streamed up to their section of the wall.

The group jogged down the stairs, heading across the busy courtyard, Daniel catching snatches of conversation even as his **Healing Aura (II)** kept washing out, healing minor nicks and aches, helping everyone within.

". . . saw it myself. Twice the size of the last one . . ."

"Siege Fireballs didn't work on it . . ."

"I hate close-quarters fighting . . ."

". . . hey, it's that Healer. Think I could get a . . ."

"Going to lose someone . . ."

"Not the prince for sure."

And then, the Master Class Adventurer was barking orders, sending them running. No time to listen, they had a job to do. And an oncoming problem that had to be solved the way all Adventuring problems got solved.

With a little steel and a lot of blood.

***

The massive siege tower that trundled up the slope—and how it did that, Daniel could only consider a matter of magic—was taller even than the walls it was meant to top. The top of the tower started showing up early, allowing the numerous Mages and Shamans stationed on top to cast their spells at the defenders. Of course, the ballista mounted on the towers fired back, but a simple shielding spell kept the tower mostly unharmed. Even inscrolled ballista bolts that punched through the **Shield** spell did little to the monster-hide-covered outer shell of the siege tower.

As for the **Fireballs**, **Ice Storms** and **Wind Blades** that the enemy Mages and Shamans cast, those were blocked or deflected by their own Mages. Daniel watched the entire proceedings with a tight-lipped grin, stuck as they were a short distance away in the middle of a tower, only able to catch glimpses through the arrow slits.

In fact, it was just the flicker of light and the howl of attacks that he mostly noticed, filling in the rest of the blanks from memory and imagination. After all, with his mediocre shooting skills, Charles would only allow him to fire from it once in a while when he had reloaded his crossbow.

"How much longer?" Roland said, shifting uncomfortably. The prince was stuck in nearly the center of the tower, protected via the crush of bodies of other Adventurers and unable to see much.

"Another five or six minutes I'd guess," Johan said, his head cocked to the side as he listened.

"How can you tell? You haven't looked up at all," Roland grumped.

"The noise."

"You can hear anything useful in all this?" Roland waved his hand around, almost knocking the head off the young fighter beside him. He had the courtesy to apologize, though the blushing female warrior who ducked her head and muttered under her breath was probably more embarrassed to be apologized to than anything else.

"It's a very distinctive sound."

"What is?"

"The approach of a siege tower," Johan explained.

"And when did you hear that?" Roland queried.

"I'm an Arms Master." Johan said, as if that explained it. And, to Daniel's surprise, it seemed to for Roland quietened.

For all of a minute before the man started complaining again. Daniel finished cranking his crossbow, waited his turn and took another shot, tuning them all out. He kind of regretted the fact that he had his **Healing Aura (II)** up. It meant that the Master Adventurer had looked at them, and then decided to pack this tower as tight as he could to make full use of the Aura.

185

Not that the twenty minutes they were stuck together was going to make that much of a difference in anything but Stamina regeneration, but Adventurers were used to eking out every little advantage they could.

Eventually though, the damn siege tower arrived. The crash and rumble of the drawbridge that they were using to both hook and open the way between the sloping edge of the tower walls and the start of the siege tower locked into place, making everyone sway and stumble a little as it did so. An abrupt, cut-off scream indicated the death knell of some poor unfortunate, and all Daniel could hope was that it was an NPC. It should be, if everyone listened to orders.

Not that there was ever a guarantee, but Adventurers learnt better. Or died early.

And then the doors slammed open, letting in fresh air. Or, at least, air that was not the mixture of scores of sweaty, bloody, unwashed Adventurers, all of them reeking of excitement and fear in equal measure. The mass of Adventurers streamed out, led by the usual teams of **Vanguards, Shield Warriors, Heavy**

Infantry and in one case, a **Southerner Warrior** to hit the wall, bowling over any in their way.

Leaving behind Daniel's team, to bring up the rear. Where, with the prince, they would be "safe."

***

"Who stealths an entire Siege Tower?" Omrak roared, his body wreathed in red aura as he held the doorway just inside the much smaller, much more angular siege tower that had appeared, just beside the bigger one. It's drawbridge had dropped just as the team had arrived, forcing them to divert to hold off the sudden surprise attack, as **Skirmishers** and **Siege Warriors** appeared. Even in the short few minutes of the fight, the Northerner had picked up a dozen wounds, and Daniel was hard pressed to keep throwing his healing spells at him and hold his side of the bridge.

"Fall back, Healer. We need you casting!" Roland barked at Daniel.

For a second, Daniel hesitated, then chose to do what the prince said. He had automatically taken the position beside Omrak, old instincts kicking in and blocking off the prince. And then, the initial press had been too busy for him to back away, before he realized that perhaps keeping the prince safe was a good idea.

But chivalry was for another time.

His blond friend was staggering, looking the worse for wear, and **Healer's Mark** alone was not enough. A quick series of **Double Strikes** drove Daniel's most recent attacker back, and then he shifted backwards, opening up a gap that another **Skirmisher** tried to duck into…only to take an arrow to the knee, sending the courageous fool stumbling off the swaying wooden drawbridge to his doom.

Roland slipped into the newly vacated place without a word, his sword weaving its way through defenses even as Omrak shuffled over further to give the Prince room to work. Daniel, finishing his spell, slapped the Northerner on the back, **Heal Medium Wounds** washing over the man, stitching his body together.

Grinning, the Northerner put his shoulder down and charged forward, taking another pair of cuts before he released his Skill, **Rage of the North** into the center of the building. Built-up lightning arced, striking both the mages and archers above and those trying to climb up the internal staircase of the building. Then, showcasing his brains rather than just bravery, the Northerner stumbled back to rejoin his friends even as Daniel weaved another spell.

And then, the fight started again. Above, Daniel could see the quick flickering motion of a black tail and a short, flipping and spinning Catkin. Rather than let their opponents rain down attacks on them, the Catkin had bounded up the siege tower herself, proceeding to draw the attention of those there. Aided by the occasional shot by Charles, she managed to keep things clear, though she was forced to do her best to pile bodies on the trapdoor to ensure reinforcements did not arrive.

Long minutes, the group fought, another Beginner Adventuring team joining them in holding the guard. It seemed like the siege tower kept spawning more and more individuals—a fact that Daniel realized was only partly true. The opening beneath the tower allowed others to climb upwards, letting them reinforce the attack.

Eyes wide with understanding, Daniel called out from his post just behind the front-line fighters. "We need to take the damn siege tower down!"

"I'm open to ideas," the Beginner Adventuring beside Daniel snapped. "My Alchemist has thrown every **Fire Potion** he has down the hatch, and none of it has caught. We've poured lamp oil down the sides, and well . . ."

He gestured, and Daniel had to agree. It had caught, but the flames weren't doing much to the monster-hide-covered siege tower.

"I got this!" Lady Nyssa cried. "Just cover me."

Glancing back, Daniel spotted the Mage moving forwards. Already, she was conjuring a **Sonic Orb** in her hand, one much larger than what she normally created. And rather than cast it away as she normally did after a few seconds, she kept channeling.

Realizing how vulnerable the woman was, Daniel scuttled backwards, putting shield in front of her. Long minutes of dealing with the occasional arrow and, in one case, a well-cast **Mana Dart** passed before she leaned over, her voice all too close to his ear, and whispered:

"On three."

Shivering, Daniel nodded. Eyes flushed, he could not help but notice how close she was, how little her protective robes really did to hide her figure. Then, the countdown was over and he stepped aside, giving her space.

At the same time as she thrust her hands forward, sending the orb spinning through the air, Daniel roared, "BACK!"

The team scrambled out of the way, running over the drawbridge even as the tower began to tremble as the **Sonic Orb** struck. Rather than disappearing or expanding, it seemed to stick to the structure, shaking the thing over and over again. Each moment, the vibrations increased in size and speed to accompany an ever-increasing scream of tortured wood.

A last, protesting scream and the entire siege tower came apart, the bonds holding it together shattered by its own vibrations. Ears still pounding, Daniel spotted a last, backflipping figure fly through the air off the top of the tower, to land on a crenelation beside him, grinning to herself as she saw the destruction.

The falling tower collapsed, knocking against the massive siege tower. Flames having taken root in the center, the weakened structure started coming apart, with the team of other Adventurers running back, or in a few cases, just teleporting back into Warmount directly.

Shaking his head, ears ringing from the sheer volume of sound even through the defensive enchantments, Daniel could not help but ask Asin.

"What kept you?"

In answer, the Catkin held up her hand, one filled with dozens of Mana stones and snatched gold chains.

Beside him, Lady Nyssa choked on a giggle, before just laughing at the greedy antics of the Catkin. Soon enough, accompanying the cheers of the victorious group were other cheers. It seemed, Daniel had to admit, their first trip to

Warmount as a team would be a rather profitable success.

Chapter 12

Johan tugged on his tunic and then collar, before his hands shifted down to his belt and pants. Before they reached, his mother was there, smacking his hands aside.

"Stop it. It took the tailors and servants ages to get it right. If you could just stop growing . . ." his mother hissed with disapproval.

Johan frowned but let her fuss, a light blush threatening to creep up his face. He did not need to turn much to see the looks the other courtiers were giving him, the way they sneered a little at the scene his mother was making, at the way he dressed.

"You . . . you know I Leveled. . . right, Ma? I . . . I had to put mmhhmm . . . more points into Strength and uh, Agility. If I'm to do my, umm . . . job . . ."

"Of course you need to do your job. I never said you shouldn't do your job. Did I say that?" His mother replied, grey eyes narrowing at the young nobleman and forced out a reluctant shake of his head. "I just wish you didn't have to keep growing. It's so . . . so . . . athletic."

"Yes, he really is, is he not?" The voice that cut across the pair's conversation made his mother and Johan stiffen, if for different reasons. His mother turned, a smile on her face of both chagrin and delight, while Johan eyed the older matriarch staring back at them. Behind her, the trio of guards that watched over the group glowered at Johan, though the Master of Arms realized he felt little fear at their regard.

Out of training, paper Levels. Those were the words that ran through his mind and that showed in his eyes as he stared back at the three, and his disdainful regard was enough for them to stiffen. Yet they said nothing, like the good bodyguards that they were.

"Johan, you haven't greeted the Viscountess Walraus," his mother said, forcing Johan to turn. He offered greetings, including the ritual bow and kiss over the hand with his usual grace, though he did note the conversation that broke out over their company.

Once he had done his greetings, his mother and the Viscountess Walraus dismissed him, nattering on about clothing and balls. He half-listened, though most of it was unimportant to him or his own concerns. Still, being forced to party with the prince and Lady Nyssa meant that he had a better grasp of most events in the capital than most.

Including . . . "I . . . I won't be . . . ummm . . . attending, uuh, Mother." Johan interrupted smoothly.

"Whyever not?" His mother turned. "Do you expect me to go alone?"

"Nuh . . . nuh . . . no. I'm . . . perhaps . . . umm . . . perhaps Lord Smith?" Johan said, somewhat placatingly he thought only for his mother to shoot him a frown. Ah, it seemed he had missed the point where his mother had moved on from Lord Smith then. "I . . . the prince. He, ummm, he invited me. To an event."

That last sentence was enough to quieten both his mother and the viscountess. There was little to be said, at least, little of substance. Not that the pair did not try to continue to speak of things, which he had to admit, drove him mad. Still, boredom and repetition was something that his martial training had offered him in spades, and this conversation, like pain, was a passing thing.

When the viscountess finally left them, Johan could not help but turn to his mother and lower his voice, even as they continued to wait in the room. He hated that they were forced to wait here, but even for nobles, bureaucracy ground on. And at least this time, they were paying off one of the imperial loans on their meager holdings rather than begging another extension. Being an Adventurer, one running Master Class and Advance Class Dungeons really was profitable.

Still. "I wish . . . wish you'd stop. Umm, speaking. With her."

"The viscountess has been a good friend to us in the past. It's always good to keep up such connections," his mother chided.

"But . . . but we don't need her. Not anymore." Johan tapped his coin pouch.

He was rather jealous of the Adventurer's **Inventory**, his own version only allowing him to store weapons and armor. On the other hand, he could equip them at a moment's notice, unlike Adventurers with their own Skill Proficiency, so there were advantages. Still, it made them hard to pickpocket, unlike him.

"And what if you, like your late father, just leave me again? How am I supposed to get by, hmmm?" his mother said waspishly.

Johan could not help but wince and lower his head a little at her correction. After all, she was right; his father's death had been the reason so much of their troubles had begun. Then again . . .

"I'm not . . . not going to . . . umm . . . die. And you know, you know, uhh, the sides. You know, which one she's on . . ." Johan muttered. "It's . . . it's bad. For us . . . to owe her."

"Oh, pish tosh. Your prince knows better than to hold that against you. And it's good to keep options open. Now, I think it's going to be our turn next, so get ready . . ."

Sighing, Johan straightened and nodded to the servant who appeared at the doorway to wave them in. It was, he decided, worth being forced to dress up in too-tight clothing to pay off another debt. Now, if they managed to keep up their current rate of earnings, he might even pay off the family's debts to the viscountess and the other noble loan sharks.

And wouldn't that be a day to celebrate?

***

"This . . . this is too much," Daniel said, eyeing the steel-and-gold bracer that was in his hand. He turned it over, again and again, his skin prickling a little at the buzz of magic that washed across his aura. This was no plain enchanted item, but a Master Work. It had been so well crafted that even his numerous enchantments that he wore interacted only subtly with it, allowing him to hold it without a concern.

"Too much, you say," the old man said, peering at Daniel from the bed he had propped himself up on. "Tell me, how often have you visited me?"

"Uhhh . . ." Daniel paused, wracking his brain.

"I do not need a full count. Just a general idea, fool child."

"Well, I guess once a week for the last three months, that'd be—" Daniel stuttered.

"Too much! And we're barely paying you for your time," the old man said grumpily.

"The amounts are negotiated with—"

"The rates are garbage. Just like your modesty. No Healer—not even Rotfield—can do what you did." The old man waved a hand at Daniel. "Any rate your guildmaster negotiated is insufficient in light of that single fact."

"I haven't cured you though, Lord Krout," Daniel said sadly.

"But you've cleared my mind, given me another three months—maybe more—that I would never have had. I've managed to clean up the house finances—something I should have done a long time ago, and don't you dare tell my son I said that. He'd never let me hear the end of that, having me admit to it." Lord Krout sighed. "You've given me time to see my grandchild grow. All of that is worth more than the handful of gold we've given you."

"But this bracer . . ."

"Is useless to my scions." Krout shook his head. "I've added more than enough items to the family vault. This one, they have no use for anyway. Not as though they go delving."

Daniel nodded a little. It was true. Krout had been one of the first Adventurers to find a new Advanced Dungeon, and with his team, had fought deep within to clear it. They had proceeded to station themselves there for the long six months before a proper Guild presence had been established, clearing the Dungeon over and over again.

In the course of such clearing, they had managed to earn their fortunes along with the bounty that the kingdom offered such location of new Dungeons. It had turned around the fortunes of the once-ailing Krout noble House and reestablished it all. And now, the Mountaindale Dungeon was run on the regular, with a small-but-growing village forming around it.

Still, all that said, Daniel turned the bracer around in his hand and peered at the information it provided once more.

Bracers of Bleeding Thorn (Master Work)

The Bracers of Bleeding Thorn is a dual-enchanted equipment with the ability to inflict minor, but consistent, damage to enemies within the aura of the wielder while siphoning and storing a small portion of its wielder's life force. This siphoned life force may be returned to the wearer upon command, creating a short-term healing effect.

Effect 1: Deals 5-7 damage per second to enemies within the user's aura.

Effect 2: Siphon and store a maximum of 47 Health Points. These Health Points may be returned to user only upon triggering of the effect.

"This is a dual-enchantment item. And a powerful one. You can't even buy this kind of work," Daniel muttered, staring at the bracer.

"No, you can't. It's a good thing I just leveled with the maker." Krout smirked. "Anyway, if you won't take it as payment, consider it insurance on my part."

"Insurance?" Daniel said.

"Of course. I need you to keep coming back, and you can't do that if you die to a bad block. Or a dagger in the dark."

"Most of my attackers come from the front," Daniel said. "And no one uses daggers in the Dungeon. You know that."

"Hah. So innocent." Krout eyes narrowed, then he shook his head after considering. "Either way. Keep it. Come back. Next week! Now, I want some roast chicken. Your healing always leaves me hungry."

Already, he dismissed Daniel, roaring his order for ale, roast chicken, and potatoes in large quantities at the servant while the Adventurer just watched. After a second more of hesitating, he made the Bracer disappear into his Inventory.

Even if the old man thought it was no big thing to give away, perhaps flaunting the new acquisition in front of his children was not the best option. He could always admire—and equip—it later. Their next run was tomorrow after all.

Offering one last nod and slight bow, Daniel saw himself out. Lord Krout was not the only individual who needed healing and who couldn't make it to the Guild Hall.

***

Asin growled low, watching the quartet of thugs stalk down the street from her perch. She sniffed a little, catching their scent, the acrid stench of old alcohol being sweated out of their pores, the lack of washing that was so common among humans. Why did humans—men especially— refuse to take proper care of their hygiene? She would never understand. She did not expect them to lick their own asses like the Caninekin, but at least wipe more than once . . . !!!

Perhaps it was just another way they chose to make life hard for Beastkin. That was, strangely, a more palatable thought than the fact that humans just chose, willingly, to walk around in that unhygienic mess that they were.

"*These three?*" Asin asked, knowing it was them. Still, better to be sure.

The young Monkeykin that hung beside her nodded, his tail wrapped around the support post. He was cradling one arm, bandaged and splinted after his latest encounter. Damn humans . . . then Asin shook her head. Not all humans, just some of them. Some were good—

like the one who promised to swing by the place after his rounds. If he did manage to make it, she'd need to make sure young Apollos beside her was seated close. Even if Daniel was out of Mana, that **Healing Aura II** could help, especially with the minor infection the Monkeykin had picked up.

But before that, she needed to handle this problem.

Judging the trio had made it far enough into the alleyway, Asin launched herself off the edge of the building, leaving the jutting roofing timber to tumble through the air. She landed with nary a sound, the simple **Cat's Grace** Skill more than sufficient to deal with the twenty-foot fall.

Behind the trio, she unsheathed her claws and moved forwards. Crouching low—and holding her breath—she struck fast and hard. Scratches across the back of legs, severing tendons and tearing skin and ligaments with the minimum of blood. The first went down almost silently, the second barely turning to see what the problem was before she took out his back leg and then had to switch to a throw.

The third was the fastest, the **Thug** swinging for the fences and nearly catching her with **Sucker Punch**. The Skill made it very hard to dodge for your average person, fooling their sense of timing and distance. Asin was not a normal person though, but an Adventurer. And high-Level **Thug** or not, he was still facing an Adventurer who faced death every other day.

She leaned back, feeling the wind of the haymaker pass her by. Then, before he could attack again, she lashed out with her claws, tearing at the arms. To her surprise, her claws slid off the skin, barely leaving a mark.

"**Hardened Skin**, fool! You think being an Adventurer means much in a fist fight?" the **Thug** snarled before lashing out with a **Flurry of Blows**.

Flipping backwards, Asin put herself out of the way of the attack, knowing that such a close combat series of blows would quickly tire him out. Then, making a quick decision, she pulled out her Amulet of Lightning, equipping it again by the simple expedient of letting it slide over her head. She shivered a little, feeling it connect with her aura once more, charging it up.

After that, the fight was pretty much over. He might be faster, perhaps even better than her in close combat. But she was in an alleyway strewn with debris and had an enchantment that allowed her thrown weapons to be charged with lightning. Lightning her opponent had no actual defense against.

Of course, she made sure to give him a good few kicks once he finally went down, cracking a couple of ribs before she sauntered out, the trio's meager purse in her hands. They would not be coming back to the Beastkin quarters any time soon.

Not that made the others happy.

"*That's the third group this week.*" The voice cut across to Asin as she was taking a seat by the roadside stall and paying for lunch for everyone with her ill-gotten gains. Best to spread the funds around fast, before they came looking for it.

"*Third group sent off too,*" Asin answered.

"*You swanning around with the prince is what brought this on us. You getting ahead of yourself, making the nobles remember we're around.*" The Boarkin that accused her sat down opposite Asin without asking, the big tusks from his chin waggling with each word. *"You should quit. They'll forget about us again, soon."*

"Not going to quit. I told you already. That's my party. Anyway, you're a fool if you think they ever forgot us. They just ignored us, because they're too busy fighting one another. But if we ever get too big, they'll just remember and tear us down."

"Exactly! And we shouldn't be rocking the boat."

"Living is rocking the boat for them," Asin snapped. *"This way, we might at least remind some of them that we're not that different. And a prince, one who likes us, can do a lot."*

"Don't be a fool, child." Another voice, this one older and kindlier.

The pair of arguing Beastkin stood up and turned to the speaker, offering deep nods of respect to the Ratkin that walked up to them. He had a staff in one hand, helping him walk along in his little brown robes. *"Expecting humans to help us is always a fool's expectations."*

Asin eyes narrowed, only for a commotion up the street to draw their attention. It was quite a distance, but even from here, Asin could catch his scent, his jovial voice as he chatted with those around. Soon enough, Asin knew, he would be down the way with his **Healing Aura (II)** turned on at full blast, offering what little aid he could to those around.

The Ratkin paused, eyes lingering at the disturbance before he turned to the smirking Catkin and added, "*As I said. A fool's expectation.*" Then, the old and stern visage softened. "But thank QuanEr for the fools."

To that sentiment, the group of Beastkin around could only nod in agreement.

Thank QuanEr indeed.

Chapter 13

"A sortie?" Daniel repeated, frowning as he stared up at the Master Class Adventurer. The man was in charge of this side of the wall—or in this case, the side of the mountain that made up the wall and portion of the fortress—and as such, was nominally in charge of the Advanced and Beginner Adventuring teams that were allocated to it. Still. "That seems rather dangerous. Especially without adequate backup."

"Are you saying my team isn't enough?" Grey eyes flashed, as the man loomed over Daniel. Being a couple of inches shorter than the average, Daniel was used to being loomed over. Not that it ever made it any more comfortable.

"No, sir. But isn't it normal for there to be at least two teams?" Daniel repeated.

"Two minimum, three recommended. Four to be safe," Johan piped up. He was normally less confident, though his stutter had slowly reduced. Not that he ever stuttered when it came time to talk about tactics or weapons.

"We're the Golden Vanguard! We're better than any two teams put together," the Adventurer snapped. "Anyway, this will be a short strike. The mine shaft they've dropped popped up within a few hundred yards of the wall, so it will be a quick sally; we'll drop the alchemical bombs into the air shaft and then retreat immediately. No reason to make it a big thing."

"If the door remains open . . ." Daniel said, glancing at the sally door they were intending to open. One of the vulnerabilities in the entire construction of the castle, but also one of the areas they could use to hit their opponents.

"There's a killing field, and the Beginner Adventurers have enough alchemicals to hold off even a Master Class team. There's also a pair of Master Class teams assigned to siege weapon four that could be here in less than a minute," the Adventurer said. "I'm not a complete fool."

Daniel wanted to protest otherwise, then chose to clamp his mouth shut. Instead, he looked over to where Roland stood, surveying the fortress.

"You people insisted you're just another Adventuring group, right? Or are you looking for handouts because you've got the prince now?"

These words were said with a sneer, making Daniel tense. Partly because he had said those exact same words numerous times to other team leaders, never wanting to receive any particular advantage. Or be held back. Now, for the first time, hearing it used against him, he realized exactly how dumb it sounded.

"I—"

"We'll do it." Roland spoke up, breaking into the conversation. "If everyone else is sallying, we'll need to be there too. Otherwise, the entire effort will truly be understrength."

"Your Highness . . ." Lady Nyssa spoke up, only for Roland to stare at her. "Roland. You know this is much riskier than anything we've done before."

"It'll be fine." Roland tapped his armor. "I'll be fine. Trust me."

Lady Nyssa looked unhappy, but a slight shake of Charles's head made her stop. She stepped back, bending her head a little in acknowledgment. That action, rather than mollify the prince just made him look even more annoyed. However, the Master Adventurer ignored the entire byplay, stalking off to deal with the next Adventuring group.

Leaving Daniel and the rest of the team to stare at one another and shake their latest disagreement off, because lingering doubts were the last thing they needed before leaving the safety of the walls.

***

Slipping out of the door was simple enough. It was not really a secretive thing they could do—everyone knew where the doors were. But due to the size of the fortress and the sheer volume of space needed to be guarded, each gate was only protected by a small force. Enough to slow down any sally, at which point more mobile troops were supposed to arrive to deal with the attackers.

Fortress Vanguards, **Shield Warriors**, **Battle Wardens**, and other front-line fighters tilted that equation in the other direction of course. The Dungeon was set up, mostly, with the idea of normal armies in play—not Adventurers with their higher Levels, their specialized Skills, and their enchanted gear. Even sandboxed by the doorway opening, they were still able to break through, disrupting the formation and opening up the way.

Then the swiftly-moving skirmishers arrived. People like Johan with his **Master of Arms** Class or Asin and her high-agility, speedy throwing knives. Other skirmishers, some with short swords, others with bone-crushing hammers were in the mix, spreading out and hammering at the Dungeon soldiers. Causing chaos, driving the opposing units back.

Till people like Daniel, Omrak, and Roland followed. They bolstered the line, melee fighters filling in in the gaps where the initial vanguard and skirmishers had created, ensuring the line did not buckle. They were strong melee fighters, but just without the particular skillsets required to establish themselves.

Once that was done, the remaining members of the parties arrived, Mages and pure Healers, ranged attackers scurrying down from the walls where they had been aiding in the battle to join the group. Within a few minutes, they had cleared the wall, barely any injuries among those who had sallied.

Then again, that was expected too.

"Move! To the mine entrance. Double time! And make sure to safeguard the alchemists!" The voice roared, the Master Adventurer standing with his team. They were offset from the main group, watching the already-reacting enemy army. Eyeing the groups that were charging forwards for proper enemies to test themselves against.

The entire sally force started running, headed directly towards their objective. Teams of fast-moving fighters swept the side, skirmishing against the occasional guard that still lived or foolishly chose to stand against them. The vanguard groups stayed together, a solid wall of force that threatened any that chose to stand in their way.

All the while, archers and mages lobbed the occasional arrow and spell at those in the distance, disrupting formations and slowing down the response time. Even then, about halfway through, the Master Adventurer called out the next set of orders.

"Teams three and four, break!"

Pivoting smoothly, the Adventuring teams thus named split off from the main sally group. They regrouped with ease, setting themselves up to face the oncoming horde. Already, the ranged fighters were unleashing a barrage of attacks, hoping to disrupt the light cavalry reaction force that had reached them first. Light glowed around a couple of lances, and as the cavalry force reached the last tens of feet, they suddenly sped up.

Momentous Charge could throw off the timing of unprepared shield walls, but in this case, the cavalry were the ones caught out. A pair of shields slammed into the ground in time, and Skill Proficiencies kicked in. **Wall of Thorns** exploded upwards from one shield edge, a conical attack that caught a trio of horses. On the other side, **Boggy Ground** took the footing of a pair of horses, making them skid and fall into the lowered tower shield. They crashed into the stocky man holding it still, forcing him back a couple of feet before his enchanted footing caught and held.

That easily, the cavalry charge was disrupted and the battle turned into a swirling melee. Skirmishers popped out from behind the vanguard shield wall while enchanted spears and arrows took riders off their horses.

Daniel watched for a few brief seconds before his attention was pulled back to the front by an insistent hand. Stuck in the center as a Healer now that they no longer required the mass of melee fighters, he was forced to run alongside the others.

The group reached the hole soon enough, corpses littering the floor around the area. They soon started to disappear, becoming the Mana stones that they were originally made from. A couple of the skirmishers scooped up the Mana stones while the rest of the teams split up, setting themselves up to deal with the fast approaching second wave of fighters. In the meantime, the Alchemist in the center with their potions hurried over to the air shaft, pulling out concoctions and mixing them together.

"Why are they mixing them now?" Daniel said, when he realized what they were doing.

"Got to." Lady Nyssa, standing beside Daniel said. "The mixtures are too volatile otherwise. You don't want to try to carry those things when it's mixed. They're too volatile even for our Inventories."

Daniel winced at that. The same reason you couldn't put anything living in the **Inventory** was also a good indicator of items or creatures one should be wary of. There were certain rocks, certain magical objects that just broke down too fast—often to the detriment of those around—for the magic of the Inventory to hold still.

"Now, come on. Focus! What is wrong with you today?" Lady Nyssa snapped at Daniel. He followed her finger which was pointing into the distance to spot the fast-moving group of enemy skirmishers charging towards them and behind, two entire troop of shield infantry. "We don't want to be here when they arrive."

"We won't be," Daniel muttered. Still, he paid attention, surveying the surroundings for additional threats.

An explosion of earth and sound a short distance to the east had him frowning, only for the dust cloud to clear to show the Master Class team caught up in an engagement with a Warg-Riding Heavy Cavalry group. The fighters on the wargs—giant, demonic wolves—were muscular and powerful, each of them wielding a trio of Skills. By themselves, they were no challenge to the Master Class Adventurers, but as an entire squad, they would certainly keep the Adventurers busy.

"They're held up," Daniel said.

"So?" Lady Nyssa said, her hands brushing against a pair of wands. She picked one, pointing it at one of the distant archers and let loose a stream of light that impacted the archer. It threw him backwards, cracking his bow and left him rolling on the ground. She cursed under her breath at not killing him, though Daniel shrugged. He was out of the fight either way.

Out of the corner of his eyes, he noted Asin rubbing at her nose, her tail moving slowly as she peered around the insides of their protective ring. He frowned, curious about what she was doing, only for his attention to be focused by Charles speaking.

"We require the Master Classers if something more . . . ah. There." Charles said with a sigh, nocking an arrow and pointing in the distance. A small rise, not so far from them, saw the appearance of a quartet of Orcs. Dungeon Orcs, similar in some ways to the native orcs of Brad, but more bestial, stronger and faster than their very own type.

Though, like the non-Dungeon kind, they were just as prone to violence.

Charles started firing the moment he finished speaking, trusting Daniel to deal with that. Lady Nyssa, frowning, was already twisting and turning her hands as she began the ritual casting of her **Sonic Orb** spell. Knowing his role—and not trusting his own aiming skills over the distance—Daniel began alerting the other ranged fighters.

A few broke off from their current targets, helping to loose their attacks upon the others. The earth erupted from underneath the running wargs, flaming arrows arced and dropped upon the orcs, and even a spinning cyclone of metal and wind tore at skin. Yet the majority of those attacks did nothing, glancing off armor, toughened skin, and almost-metallic fur. The few that did strike left light streaks of blood on the Orcs, only managing to enrage them further.

"Incoming Master Class threat on the right flank!" Daniel roared when he realized that the ranged attackers were not going to be enough to stop them. The fact that other attackers were piling in now, light and medium cavalry reaching the line kept the teams from focusing entirely on the Orcs.

Daniel's team, conditioned to respond to him, moved in close. Omrak strode forwards, taking his space in front of the group and hefting his sword. His eyes glowed as he stared at the quartet of wolves, his lips peeled back. Around him, a light red glow began to deepen in shade as he triggered a Skill Proficiency, artificially increasing the rage ability. It would cost him, later.

Prince Roland shook his head before turning to Daniel and saying wryly, "You can tell me you told me so later. Now, I'll show you why I wasn't as worried. But . . . I told you so."

Then he stepped forwards, right up to Omrak, and whispered to the Northerner. Omrak turned, looking down at the shorter melee fighter before he reluctantly nodded, stepping back. Johan took his place on the other side of the prince, having returned his paired swords to his inventory and pulling out a massive polearm with a long blade on the end. He hefted the weapon easily, stepping far enough away from the prince that he could wield it easily, while not endangering those behind or to the side. Not that many chose to stand near the Master of Arms when he wielded that weapon.

Another team broke off, filtering over to join their group, taking up the edge near Omrak. Unlike their own team, this one contained three front-line fighters and a pair of skirmishers, the front-line fighters wearing similar gear in the short spear and shield combo they used and the skirmishers having slightly more varied weaponry. One had even exchanged his normal smaller mace for a larger warhammer, hefting the weapon with a grin. Catching Daniel's look and

222

his own much smaller blunt weapon, the man grinned.

"Best way to crack an Orc, eh?"

Daniel wanted to answer, but that was when Lady Nyssa finally chose to release her **Sonic Orb**. That spell had been charged for long minutes, such that it was a densely packed, warped sphere of energy that howled as it flew forwards as swiftly as an arrow.

Instincts had the wargs and their riders split apart, leaving a gap in their charge. However, to their surprise—and Daniel's—the spellwork twisted in midair, following the side near Omrak to strike the nearest monster. Detonating, it unleashed its energy in a singular pulse of vibrations, blowing ears and disrupting balance and tearing apart skin and organ within. Warg and Orc collapsed and the other rider on that side collapsed, his beast rolling around the ground in agony, leaving him steedless.

However, that was not the end of the fight. While annoyed by the spell, the other trio of Orcs bore down on the team, intent on rolling over Johan. The Master of Arm's face grew tight but determined as he crouched low, ready to strike.

Only for a blazing streak of orange and gold to pass him by as Roland triggered his armor's ability. Like a meteor, he impacted the lead rider, bowling the larger and more muscular orc and the demonic wolf over. The crash and the crunching of bone and skin echoed through the battlefield, and only the ear numbing effect of the earlier Sonic Orb was a good comparison.

The Orc that had been impacted bounced away with his Warg, the pair splitting up as they flew through the air. They lay, unmoving, bones jutting from skin as Roland spun towards the pair of remaining Orcs, only now recovering from his explosive arrival.

The team moved forwards, breaking from the line to backup Roland, Daniel snarling a little at the prince's impetuousness. He could have sworn he had beaten it out of the boy before now!

A mighty swing, massive cavalry sword coming down onto raised shield. It flared with power, taking on a golden sheen just like

Roland's armor and blocked the assault with contemptuous ease. The weapon bounced off, and Roland swung his own blade, cutting lightly into the extended arm. A Warg, moving fast and low, came from the side, monstrous, diamond-tipped teeth clamping down on the thigh. Only to be rebuffed by the enhanced armor aura, teeth scrabbling and unable to find purchase.

A kick punted the monster away, even as Roland triggered a new skill. One that Daniel knew, if only having seen it occasionally. **The Kingdom's Strength** was a Royal Skill Proficiency, one that increased the prince's strength by significant amounts, so long as the kingdom itself was whole. And it was.

Armor fully triggered, his Legendary weaponry and Skills at play, Roland went to work, taking apart the remaining two Master Level Orcs and their Wargs, holding them off and even winning. Meanwhile, Johan and Omrak were off to the side, fighting with the aid of Charles and Lady Nyssa against a group of medium infantry in their chain armor and their swords and shields, tearing down their shield walls to allow the other two to finish the fight.

Daniel caught all this as he ran, closing in on the prince, knowing that his main job was to keep him safe. However, he slowed for a brief moment, realizing someone was missing. He tilted his head, spotting Asin, who had stopped in her dash over to the other group and was staring, at him and the prince.

Then, she had knives in her hands and he was not seeing anything anymore as he was struck, once and then again.

Chapter 14

Asin sniffed, turning her head from side to side. That smell was there again, cinnamon, nightshade, and weapon oil. It was an unusual combination, and for some reason, it set her fur on end. It kept appearing and disappearing since the fortress and for the life of her, she could not figure out where it was coming from. No matter how she looked or sniffed, she could not find it.

Another shout, this time from Daniel, and she shook her head, dismissing thoughts of the vagrant smell. The Master Level Orcs on their Wargs were coming, and she no longer had time to worry about such things.

Of course, the next few seconds put that entire concern to rest. Even as she was shaking off the effects of Lady Nyssa's **Sonic Orb**—and was that annoying, especially when she increased its strength like she had—the prince had jumped into battle, making himself a target.

He also put himself in further danger by attracting the attention of the medium infantry troop that had been going for the line of Adventurers, instead diverting to them. Daniel, of course, noted that problem and had snapped out orders, making Omrak and Johan, who were headed to guard the prince more directly, change course.

She was following along with them, keeping a decent distance back since she was not a lunk-headed idiot with too many muscles and not enough sense, when she caught that scent again. Instinct—**Bestial Instinct**—pulled at her, and she turned, searching. Her eyes drifted towards Daniel and the prince, both of them caught up in a swirling dust cloud that had risen from the initial prince's impact and the Warg's running around the pair.

Something was there . . . something that made her hackles rise. That made her grip her throwing knives harder than ever and that screamed at every instinct.

Dust moved and shifted around the pair. Swirling clouds of soil that flowed around them. Without a breeze. Daniel was turning to her when Asin realized what was happening. Two, no, three dust clouds—one near Daniel, two others near the embattled prince who had just finished embedding his sword in a Warg, pinning it to the ground.

She had a choice to make.

It was never a choice.

Her hands flashed forwards, Stamina and Mana pouring down her hand as she threw her knives. **Penetration** combined with **Fan of Knives.**

Too late.

She watched the assassins appear from thin air, their blades punching forwards. The first caught Daniel in the side, just under his ribs. It hit him once and then again before the Healer collapsed to the ground. Shifting position, the assassin aimed for his throat.

Only to find itself pin-cushioned by her attack. The weapons tore into his light armor, one impacting the raised arm and forcing the killer to drop his weapon. Other knives burrowed into his body, making him jerk and twist as the lightning enchantment in her aura delivered its shocks. It would slow him down only for a few seconds, Asin knew.

Not that the Catkin was waiting. She sprinted across the bare earth, unleashing a loud, angry yowl to alert the rest of the team. In her peripheral vision, she saw the other two assassins on Prince Roland, their daggers red in blood. Another flash, as a protective enchantment went off, only to be combatted by their own Skills and enchantments.

Then, she no longer had time to watch. Sprinting on all fours, she leapt one last time, throwing herself at the recovering assassin and bearing him to the ground. Together the pair tumbled, the light Catkin twisting and riding the fall to end up on top. Her daggers appeared in her hand as she began to stab it into her opponent, only to find him struggling and fighting.

Thrown off his body, the Catkin flipped through the air to land on her feet. A dart, thrown with great force, punched through her armor and deflective enchantments, tearing into a shoulder and removing her ability to use one arm.

No matter.

The Catkin moved forwards, ducking low and kicking out, only to see the other man dodge her attack with contemptuous ease. Eyes wide, Asin realized she might just be outmatched.

Even with the numerous wounds she had inflicted, the other man was moving, and moving well.

Jade eyes narrowed, and Asin let out a little yowl, crouching low. This was not going to be a fast fight in either case. She could only hope that the prince could survive on his own.

***

Roland cursed, feeling blood pouring down one side. Legendary armor had been pierced like it had been nothing more than cloth. The daggers his assassins had wielded had disintegrated upon use, dissolving in his chest and dumping the poisons they held within into his body. He could feel it pumping through his veins even now, attempting to stop his heart, attempting to freeze his muscles.

Royal Constitution was keeping it at bay, a secret Skill Proficiency. Similar in some ways to **Warrior's Health** or **Soldier's Hardiness**, it was a restricted Skill Proficiency but was significantly more powerful, if more limited. It did less to improve his overall health unlike the

231

other two named Skills—or a Beastkin's **Bestial Ancestry**—but it did provide a much, much higher level of protection against more subtle threats. Like diseases. And poisons.

He needed time to take some of the antidotes he had been given, but the assassins weren't letting up, forcing him to pay attention to their movements. They were fast too, much faster and more skilled than even the Orcs and Wargs. With a single Warg and Orc left each, they were making the entire battle a mess, with the pair launching attacks at the assassins and Roland indiscriminately.

Another blurring movement to his left. His shield yanked him sideways, the **Flawless Parry** enchantment triggering to pull him off balance to block the strike. Unfortunately, the other assassin knew what was about to occur and launched himself in a low lunge, new dagger seeking the gap between his cup and thigh armor.

Only for Roland to trigger another enchantment in his sword, **Lightning Counterstrike**. His sword flickered forwards and down, slicing off the extended hand and then flicking back upwards in a backhand strike to seek his neck. However, off balance and pulled aside by the enchantments, Roland neither had the speed nor stability to follow through that attack properly. He was just a touch too slow as the now-handless assassin fell back, clutching his arm but still silent.

However, for that brief moment, he was paying attention entirely to Roland. He never saw the Warg that took his neck from behind, pulling him down to the ground, jaws clamped on the back of his neck as it twisted and turned his neck. A sharp crack echoed through the clearing, signifying the man's death. Dropping the corpse, the Warg threw its head back to howl its victory only to stagger at the movement, and then for its eyes to roll backwards entirely and fall down, dead.

"Poison," Roland snarled, his attention once more focused on the other assassin. He had picked up his movements again, another enchantment in the helm giving him the Perception to keep the slinking Master Class in sight.

No answer. Not that Roland expected the assassin to make a mistake like that to engage him in speech. Only foolish beginners did that. Foolish like him. He should have kept to the line instead of trying to show off. Now, he was caught out in the middle, his party was split up and fighting multiple enemies and he was bleeding to death and poisoned.

Idiot. He never learnt. No matter how many times Daniel or Lady Nyssa or his father told him . . .

He blinked, staring down as pain erupted in his chest. Another dagger, planted in him. The assassin was up next to him now, his blade deep in Roland's body, twisting it. He could the assassin's bearded face now, the smirk. And he realized what happened—a mental skill. Something like **Distracted Thoughts** or **Idle Musings**. Merchants and politicians had skills like that, and so it seemed did assassins.

He fell backwards, pain taking him. Only grateful that the Legendary armor had managed to shift the attack point away from his heart to his lungs. Now he'd die slower. Though, even as he fell, a last enchantment triggered.

Lightning rushed down the arm, crisping the attacker, ending him.

Leaving but the Master Class Orc the holder of the field, confused and angry and stalking over to the prone prince.

***

Daniel curled up around his body, pain washing everything out of his mind but the injury, the poison, and his Gift. It worked automatically, stealing away memories, stealing away his experience to fix the poison. Yet it was not enough. The amount being pulled from him was more than he had ever experienced at one go, as though the poison itself was hungry for his experience, his healing. He kept pouring it in, and it was working, but it was taking its toll.

The sounds of battle slowly filtered through his senses as the poison and wounds closed. He could hear the clash of swords, the grunt of pains, and the screams of the dying along with the occasional filtered curse. Omrak was loud as always, and the discordant shriek of Lady Nyssa's sound magic was comforting, in a painful way. He could not hear Asin, but that was normal.

As for Roland . . .

Breathing stopped for a second, when memory flooded in. Panic threatened to rise and carry him away, but Daniel fought it down. He had to get up, he had to heal himself. Now. The prince was injured, and if he died . . .

If he died, it would all be Daniel's fault. He should never have insisted they come here. They should never have left the walls of the fortress. They should never have let him go out by himself.

Fool.

Another surge of energy, something precious and soft ripped itself from Daniel's memory. He caught a glimpse of it as it went: *laughing Beastkin faces, dyed in red and white, the smell of spices and taste of hot food as the bells for QuanEr rang through the neighborhood. Kinship and wonder, all in one as he found himself with those who saw him for more than just a miner or Healer, who just wanted his company and . . .* then it was gone.

Leaving nothing but an ache and his wounds closed, the poison robbed of its vitality. Daniel pushed himself to his feet, his gaze panning over the surroundings. Asin, thrown from a side kick, hit the ground and rolled not far from him, the figure that hit her fading out of sight even as he retracted his foot. He was focused entirely on the Catkin, bleeding a little but still alive. Still fighting.

Roland, not so far away, standing still and moving slowly. Sword waving around in midair, as though he was looking for the fighter that was right in front of him. The others just about finishing off the infantry group, Charles turning already to seek additional threats, an arrow nocked.

A brief consideration, but Asin was not moving and they needed the threats down. He could heal Roland's injuries, if he was still standing. If he ran over now, the threat at his back could take him down while he ran. Better to deal with this assassin now.

He pushed himself to his feet, pushing his shield back to line up properly with the edge of his hand as he got his feet under him. A brief moment of vertigo, squashed by Gift and stubbornness. Too late though, for the signs of the killer going after the Beastkin was gone.

But . . .

Asin might not be getting to her feet just yet, but she was watching the ground, focused. Daniel tracked the way her eyes moved, where she looked and took off running. He could only hope that he guessed right, even as he strained his own Perception to the maximum. If he could see him . . .

He couldn't. But the shield he held in front of him was smacked aside long before he crashed into the other. Then, a stinging sensation as the hammer he gripped in his hand was knocked out of his grip. Still, his momentum was barely diverted, and Daniel used the attacks to change his footing just a little to the now-revealed opponent. He dove into the other, wrapping splayed arms around the man and taking him to the ground.

The assassin squirmed and twisted, already levering Daniel upwards, heavy plate armor or not. He was very skilled, and Daniel felt another blade slide into a gap just above his hip. He groaned as it bit in, more poison delivered. But it didn't matter.

He got a hand around the man's arm, and that was all he needed. Daniel dove into his Gift, ignoring the pain, the way he was twisted and thrown to the side, the blade ripping free as he was cast aside. The other man tried to pull away, but Daniel's grip was locked tight, and he had enough time.

First, spasm the muscles, making them clench tight. An automatic response, one that forced the other man to curl into a bowl. Then, deeper, dumping certain substances, chemicals that he had noticed deep within a body, that froze people tight, that caused them to shut down. He'd sensed it in the truly injured, the scared or the ones in pain. He used to take it away, stop the production.

This time, he increased it till his opponent stopped moving. Rather than let it taper off, Daniel made sure to keep it running. He would not kill, but shutting down a killer's ability to move, to think, to fight? That he would do.

Taking his hand off the other, he used his **Medium Wounds** spell on himself, letting the magic patch him together mostly. Injuries he picked up, including a cut across his neck that he had not even noticed happening and another across the arm threaded close and clotted.

Good enough for now.

A flicker of information, a notification swirled up in his eyes. He shuddered, seeing the numbers, but pushed them away a second later.

*Level Loss * 3*

Then Daniel was on his feet, Asin joining him a moment later, still limping. They both turned, only to see the prince lying on the ground, dagger still in his chest, his attacker dead. Smoke rose from the pair, a byproduct of the exchange of energy and the enchantment.

Finally, they spotted the last Master Class Orc stalking over to the prone prince, rage on his face.

Chapter 15

Charles nocked and fired, loosing the arrow and burying it in the earhole of the human infantryman that had chosen to focus on Omrak. Somewhere in the battle, he had lost his helmet, leaving the bobkin head to bury itself in the skull without a problem.

A casual step backwards gave Charles further view of the surroundings, enough that he could look for additional problems in the line. However, both Johan and Omrak had the matter well in hand, with his charge laying waste to the last of a pair of scouts, holding aloft the wand of **Mana Arrows** to conserve her Mana. Not that she likely had much left, not after her showing against the Master Class Orcs.

A little portion of Charles glowed with pride at the memory. The much larger, more professional portion scanned the surroundings, already recalling the other problem even as he nocked another arrow. And there he was, lying on the ground, barely alive.

Idiot child.

Charles eyes narrowed a little, seeing the Orc. Eyes flicked between the players on the battlefield, those that he had noticed and those that might still be in play. He debated his options, his duty to the Lady and to the House, and then drew the arrow to his cheek. He sighted it along the line of march and then loosed, instilling **Penetration** into the arrow.

It would harm the Orc, and if he was lucky, end him. But chances of that happening was almost nothing. No, something else had to be done. And it seemed, it would be up to him to do it.

Arrow loosed, Charles stored the bow and drew his sword in a smooth motion, sprinting forward. There was a skill; any good bodyguard had it. He just needed to get close enough to trigger it, and thankfully, the swirl of battle had pulled them all close.

Now, he just had to wait . . . just a little.

Close enough to watch the Orc take the arrow in its shoulder, to turn and snarl at him. To briefly consider killing him, before it turned back to Roland and took the last few steps. Time enough for him to close the distance more, still behind the pair of Adventurers loping forwards, throwing knives in the air between the pair.

He hoped they didn't hit him when he—

A sword swung down.

And his Skill triggered.

Bodyguard's Sacrifice was not an actual sacrificial attack. He didn't take the damage onto his body, nor did it require him to suffer. It just put him in the right place at the right time, so that he could block a blow. With sword or body—the Skill did not care.

Of course, he still had to cross the distance; which was why it had a certain range. It drained him of Stamina and Mana when it warped him over, yanking him across the space in nearly instantaneous movement, making his shoulders ache and his hip hurt where a damn throwing knife had embedded itself in him as he passed it by.

But he was in the way, and the sword was blocking.

Timed perfectly.

Except for the fact that this was a Master Class Orc. And he was but a poor bodyguard.

The blade crashed through his guard, embedded itself in his chest and drove itself all the way down to his heart. He could feel it

243

stagger and stop, his eyes widening. Then, Charles grinned, savagely.

One last act, then. **Repentance** unleashed, an enchantment on his necklace, passed down his family. He hoped his son would remember why he did this, why they chose to save others when they could have lived. He hoped Lady Nyssa made sure to keep her promise. Not that the House had ever betrayed them.

Then, all the pain, all the damage was returned to the Orc.

And finally, finally they both fell.

***

"Noooo!" Daniel screamed, jogging forwards as fast as he could. Not fast at all, not quick enough to make a difference. Not anymore. He made it to the crumpled form of Charles, the damnable sword ripped from his body when the orc fell. If it had been left within, maybe he could have done something. But it hadn't, and the blood had gushed out from the open wound, and now, it was barely dribbling.

His Gift was powerful. It was something that could fix, that could heal everything. His **Healing Aura II** was already at work, but as hand came into contact with cooling flesh, he could sense that it was barely doing anything. Barely.

It was enough.

He dove deep within, pushing at the power that was his. In the distance, he could hear a scream, sobbing sounds arising from Lady Nyssa. He knew what it was for, what it was about, but he refused to acknowledge it. Daniel had not the time.

. . . fix the heart first, patch it together so that it could beat . . . blood vessels, torn and ruptured, had to get those before restarting the heart . . . body temperature was falling, body going into shock. Had to change that, push the body to warm itself, stop production of those chemicals there . . . torn muscles didn't matter . . . had to string those two veins together, the artery to one another . . . heart, start it now or else it's too late . . .

Charles was fading away. Daniel could tell, he could feel him drifting away with each passing second. He worked as quickly as he could, the **Healing Aura II** he used managing to,

245

thankfully, slow down the degradation. It couldn't fix anything, not at all, but it helped. Enough at least, for him to find the minimum that he needed to finish this. Then he just needed to restart the heart . . . cast a spell . . .

Memories rushed away. So many. Khy'ra, sharing kisses and laughter in bed. His grandfather, showing him to wield a pickaxe for the first time. Long hours, in the mines, hammering away. A memory, a stolen kiss from a young girl, around the corner from the cookfires. Nights in the inn, dreams remembered and then . . . gone.

Not enough. The heart began to beat again, and Charles almost lurched upwards. Daniel pushed back down, already calling up his magic. Only for a hand to land on his shoulder, forcing him to turn away.

"What?"

"The prince. You have to heal the prince," Lady Nyssa said, her eyes conflicted, her hands pouring a healing potion onto Charles open wound. It started closing, fixing some of the damage. There was only so much the potion could do, but it was doing it.

"I have to . . ." Daniel said, gesturing at Charles.

"Will he last?" Lady Nyssa snapped.

Daniel paused, looking down at the closing wounds, at the pale face. He had fixed the traumatic damage, patched the other together. Bones still were broken, muscles cut apart. But the major parts were holding together, patching a bit.

Seeing the answer before he even spoke, Lady Nyssa pulled at Daniel with surprising strength. "Then fix the prince. I have him."

"Bandage and splint him!" Daniel commanded as he turned away. "And no more healing potions."

"I know!"

Then, he had no more time. The prince was there, on the ground. They had not pulled the dagger out, though Asin had placed cloth around the wounds in an attempt to stem the bleeding. There was a lot of blood on the ground, not a lot left coming from him.

Gritting his teeth, Daniel knelt once more, to take hold of the prince's hand. Only to find himself swaying and almost falling over. Only the grip of Omrak, whose sudden appearance surprised the Healer, kept him from falling over.

Lying in the other man's hand, Daniel frowned. There was no reason, no . . .

"Shit. The poison." The second one, that he had been dosed with. He hadn't healed that, hadn't fixed that in his own body. His Gift went inwards, finding it, crushing it. When he came back, long seconds later, a notification he had been ignoring was flashing before him. Updated once again.

Level Loss * 4
Note: Marty's Touch has been overused in a short period. Further use is not recommended. Permanent damage may occur.

Eyes wide, Daniel waved the notification away. He had no time, not for this. Pulling away from Omrak, he bent downwards, hand plunging down to make contact with the quiet prince. He played over his options, staring at the knife in the man's chest, then sent his Gift questing for further information.

Damaged lung. Chest cavity filling with blood, though slowly. Still, restricting his breathing. Blood loss was significant, causing the heart to struggle. A **Medium Healing** spell could help take care of that, though in some ways his **Healing Aura II** was actually causing trouble, forcing the body to attempt to heal itself when its own resources were deeply damaged. Puncture wounds including a damaged kidney on one side and the nicked veins in the upper left chest from the initial attacks. Three types of poisons. One was already being driven out, Roland's basic poison resistance more than sufficient. The other two were a problem. One was a soul eater, the very same kind that he had dealt with in his own body—but the prince had double the dosage. And that poison had time to travel through his body. The second was a simpler one, intent on attacking the nervous system of the prince and shutting it down.

So.

Memories shifted, disappearing. Something about Asin . . . a talk with her about boys. Cats? Wait, Daniel wanted to scream, it was important. But it was gone, long before he could touch it. Another memory shifted, detaching, and for a second, he struggled with understanding what he saw in the poisons. Medical knowledge had always been relatively safe from his Gift, almost as though Erlis knew he needed it to use his Gift properly. But this time . . .

This time it was all going.

Daniel shivered, breaking clear of his thoughts, pulling back for a second. He lifted his hand from the other, staring down at the unmoving body.

"Why aren't you doing anything?" Joshua snapped.

"I need to think . . ."

"About what? Just use your Gift!"

"It's not that simple," Daniels said. "There's multiple injuries and poisons. I can't just . . ." He shook his head, looking around for a second. "Triage."

"What?" Johan said.

"Friend Daniel means that he will stabilize the prince first. Then finish the healing later," Omrak rumbled. "We are in danger out here. We must bring him back, fast."

As though to punctuate Omrak's words, there was an explosive rumble. The group turned as one to watch as harsh smoke billowed out of the mine airhole, growing darker and forcing the Adventurers around it back.

"Quickly," Asin snapped.

Nodding, Daniel bent and began the healing. Fix what had to be fixed first. First, isolate and contain the poisons. The neural-toxin had to be dealt with first, otherwise the prince would not survive the more dangerous, but slower-acting soul poisons. Those were spreading without being countered, but were a lesser danger for now. The failing nervous system and struggling heart had to be dealt with.

He patched the wounds, sewing together veins and arteries the same way he had fixed his own wounds, a slapdash effort that would leave scars. Muscles were pulled together, pushed together at parts before he reached for the dagger. A single yank had it pulled out, and then blood gushed.

"Ba'al's Curse!" Johan cursed.

"It's fine," Daniel muttered, ignoring the conversation around him.

Something about strapping Charles to a gurney to be carried, and arguments about just carrying him physically over Omrak's shoulders. He ignored it all, pushing the blood that had collected in the chest cavity out, until it was mostly gone. Then he finished closing the lung, leaving the open chest wound.

A step backwards, an Inventorying of the dagger. He cast a **Heal Medium Wounds** on the prince, borrowing Mana's ability to work miracles to close wounds and even create blood. Again, a second later, he cast it, and then he traced his hand on the body.

Seconds later, he looked up and nodded to the group. "Let's move."

"About time!" Omrak said, rumbling. He bent down, scooping up Roland in his arms across his chest, before looking at Lady Nyssa. The Mage had just finished stuffing another potion down Charles's throat and to everyone's surprise, he had staggered to his feet. Looking much worse for wear, but standing.

"Johan," Asin called out, pointing the way they had to go. Through a group of fast-moving skirmishers who were coming for them, even as other teams moved to block the way of other incoming groups. Even the Master Class team seemed to have realized the situation and were in the process of providing cover for the team.

After all, no one wanted to be implicated in the death of a prince.

"We run," Johan said, dropping the visor on his helmet and starting a slow jog, his weapons and armor shimmering as he switched them out for his favorite pair of swords.

They ran.

Chapter 16

Daniel lurched and tottered along behind the group, his mind numb and tired. Days and months later, he would find himself unable to properly recount the passage, the chaos of battle and the effects of his Gift taking its toll on his recollection. More so, his exhaustion from his earlier usage and his still-healing injuries drove him to distraction, such that he was of little use to the fight.

Rather, he ran behind his team, accompanying Omrak and lending aid to the group with his **Healing Aura**. Somewhere along the way, he had lost a Level and the ability to use the Skill at a higher level. He knew, deep within him, that something had changed in his Gift, something had broken in the repeated and harried usage. Even now, he could not help but wonder how many of his Skill Proficiencies still worked. **Shield Bash** was gone, the shield on his hand a lump that felt unnatural in his hand. Too many moments of training, too much of his life memories withdrawn. There were others, he knew that he had lost.

Erlis giving him a chance to keep some of his healing skills. But he couldn't remember, couldn't recall what he did at the clinic back at Silverstone. The days there were hazy now, the faces half-remembered. Instances and cases were starker, the symptoms he used to diagnose clearer. The people . . . faceless.

Something hit him in the side and he stumbled to the side, falling to the ground. He struggled to his feet, shaking his head, combat instincts faded. The second strike caught him on his breastplate, staggering him upwards and driving the air out of still full lungs.

He swung his fist, feeling it connect and bounce off. For a moment, he wondered where his hammer was. Then another strike from the sword-wielding attacker took him back down to his knees. Daniel caught the return attack on a raised shoulder, sending the blade skittering off the pauldron and onto his helmet, ringing his head but leaving him mostly unharmed.

Shocked, perhaps. But unharmed.

Then, a fast-moving, dark blur hit the attacker from the side, coming in low and wrapping itself around the fighter. Daggers flashed, limbs twisted and tossed and the fighter fell to the ground, the Catkin crouched over him.

255

A dagger dove downwards, stabbing deep into a neck and then exited.

By this point, Daniel was on his feet. He had a hand up, ready to punch—why was he punching? Where was his hammer? —but the Catkin was just staring at him, crouched low. Her ears swiveled back and forth as she turned her head, whiskers flicking in the wind.

"Run!" the Catkin—Asin! that was her name—barked.

Daniel ran.

He wished he knew what was the problem, why he could not seem to understand what was happening. His head spun every couple of minutes, the flow of the battle constantly frustrating him.

Ahead, a boy with two swords was carving his way through a pair of attackers that had escaped past another Adventuring team. He literally jumped and spun through the air, his swords held outwards as they cut across throat and through armor like butter.

Then, another stumble, a hand pulling him up by the elbow. An older man, looking worse than Daniel himself felt, pulled him up. Beside them, the Mage turned and ran backwards, her robes flapping at her legs as she raised her hand. A shield, one that vibrated and twisted the very air, making the Healer—that was what he was, a Healer—vibrate.

Incoming arrows bounced off the shield, some empowered attacks diverted as the shaft of the arrows they held cracked apart under the vibrations. They still fell, but off course and deflected as they were, they were significantly less dangerous. A few Skills, requiring the entire arrow to work, even flickered and died, leaving the attacks no more dangerous than, well, a hail of arrows.

"Lady Nyssa, you must hurry!" the older gentleman called back, urgently.

"I will. But this time, it will be me who guards you! Run, or else I won't be coming either."

Frustrated, the older man chivvied Daniel along. He shook his head, pushing aside the byplay, focusing ahead. More enemies were coming, some riding horses, others giant wolves. Infantry clashed with the Adventurers, as the group ran for their lives, the walls of Warmount looming ahead but still seeming so far. Explosions from spells, the ringing of weapons on armor and the screams of the dying rang through the mountain constantly. It was bedlam, and Daniel's mind shrank a little from it all even as his soul crowed and glowed.

"War Champions arriving from the south!" A hoarse shout, one filled with fear, caught their attention.

"How many?" Another voice. Arrogant, idiotic, foolish voice. Daniel was irritated just hearing it, though he couldn't remember why.

"Half dozen."

"Ba'al's tears." The words were said as a curse, but softly. It still carried through the battlefield in a trick of sound and circumstance. There was a long pause, then the voice rose, this time louder and firmer. "Maximum Force—to me! We hold the Champions till the prince is safe. Use everything. Don't hold anything back."

More movement, more people streaming. He noticed a group break away, joining the newly formed Maximum Force. Words were being exchanged, a lot of gestures thrown around.

Daniel was forced to look away, to focus on his running, his breathing labored.

Stamina was good, so why was he panting? Why was his heart beating like the stretched skin of an Orc's war drum? Why did he even know what an Orc war drum sounded like? He had never heard one, had he? He'd never been in a war.

Gaps.

Too many gaps.

And noise, coming from behind him now. Screams and roars, the roar of explosions and the hum of magic coming to life. The sky darkened behind Daniel, eve as the postern door was thrown open and other Adventurers streamed out, some moving to guard him—him? Why was he being guarded—and others to the still figure in the giant blond man's arms.

Even more figures were appearing above the wall, including an elf with long hair, hauling back on an oversized bow. Aiming into the distance and loosing an arrow that was made of blue light and green, that seemed to flicker to life as a giant cat formed around it. Then it was off, streaking through the sky and above him.

He ducked, feeling his soul quail at its passing. A hand gripped his arm, he was pulled in further and then, suddenly, he was hearing the word "safe."

Somehow, he didn't feel safe. He just felt confused.

***

"What's wrong with him?" a voice snarled, a finger pointing.

Lady Nyssa took her time answering, pulling her Mage robes down and smoothing them out. She glanced over at Daniel, the "him" being asked about, and then spoke, calmly. You had to be calm, especially when everyone else around you was not. Even if your heart was thudding in your chest like it would rip itself out and spill all your secrets. Even when you were not certain. Especially when you were not certain.

"Daniel has used his Gift significantly. To heal himself, Charles, and to stabilize the prince. I fear he is paying the Price for his indiscriminate use."

The Royal Bodyguard shrunk a little at the word Price. Everyone knew that those so Gifted had a Price to pay. Sometimes it was their health. Sometimes it was their lifespan. Other times, it was even more esoteric. But there was always a Price.

Even so, he shrugged away the socially constructed fear, duty overriding it all. "The prince lies unconscious, his wounds barely tended. The other Healers have cast healing spells to no effect. They say he was poisoned." A pause, a deeper breath. "If he was attacked by the assassins like you said, then whatever his *Gift* does, it can fix the prince too."

"I know," Lady Nyssa said. "But he needs a few minutes."

"The prince might not have that!" the Royal Bodyguard snapped.

"And if he makes a mistake?"

That dire comment had the man freeze for he understood what that might mean. After all, a Healer was what he was because of his ability and knowledge. A confused Healer was as much a danger to the patient as whatever ailed him.

"Fine. He can have . . ." The man paused, turning, and fixed his gaze on one of the nearby Healers. When the man returned the stare, he made an impatient sound.

"Uhh . . . maybe a few hours. He's stabilized, and mundane healing has kept the wounds from reopening and clotted. The poison is stable for now, but . . ." A shrug. "I just don't know. I've never seen anything like it before."

The bodyguard nodded, staring back at Lady Nyssa. "You have an hour. Get him calm. Get him ready."

Lady Nyssa nodded, and walked off to Daniel. Nearby, Asin was seated beside Daniel, who was looking better, less panicked as he chewed on the roll of meat and bread that she had handed him. Her eyes watered as she neared the pair, the spices from the meat making her wince.

It was a strange feeling, being around so many others without her shadow. Charles had been taken away by the waiting Healers the moment they had arrived in Warmount, the man almost ready to collapse. She had watched them take him away, and only arrived late to see the burgeoning problem with the Royal Bodyguard. Now, now, she finally had time to breathe.

And worry.

For all that she had tried to reassure the bodyguard, there was something seriously wrong with Daniel. He was not acting like himself. She had seen him concussed, seen him stabbed and crushed and under pressure and she had never seen him like this.

Squashing the fear within herself, she spoke softly and gently to the pair. "Daniel? How are you doing?"

"I'm . . . I'm better." Daniel shook his head. "I'm sorry, I wanted to thank you. For the . . . the . . . **Sonic Wall**?" Some of the confusion cleared up as he recalled the name. "Yes. **Sonic Wall**."

"No thanks needed between party members," she said.

"We're party members?"

Asin nodded, then raised a finger and pointed. "Omrak."

"I remember him. He's . . . wearing a shirt?" Daniel paused, confused.

Asin grinned, letting out a little chuff of laughter while Lady Nyssa just looked confused. She shook her head, dismissing the incongruity. Why would any Adventurer be delving without a shirt?

"Lady Nyssa." Pointing to her, Asin continued. Finger tracked to the side of the woman. "Shadow—Charles."

"Her shadow is named Charles?"

"My bodyguard is named Charles."

"Oh, right!" A nod. "The older man. He looked bad. Minor concussion, remnant poison and blood loss. Wounds weren't fully healed and he reopened them on the run."

"Exactly!" Lady Nyssa said, happy to see something of his old expertise returning. Or at least, still in play.

"And the last one . . . Josh?" Daniel said, tentatively. The Masters of Arms was standing, nervously, in the corner. No longer in battle, he kept shifting from side to side, uncomfortable in the presence of so many.

"Johan." Lady Nyssa corrected gently.

"Right. Right. And we were in a team with a . . . Roland. And he was important."

"Yes, he was."

Then, eyes widening, Daniel bolted upright. "I remember! I have to finish healing him."

Lady Nyssa let out a relieved breath, at the same time Asin let out a low yowl, clawed hands clamping down on an elbow. Daniel paused, looking at the Catkin.

"You. Bad. Must stop."

"I'm fine."

"No."

"I'm fine."

"No."

"I'm—"

"NO." The Catkin stood up, waving her hands around. "NO. You broken. Heal. Break further."

"I have to do this," Daniel said. Confused as he was before, there was a thread of iron in his voice at he made the statement.

Lady Nyssa, watching the pair of argue cleared her throat.

"Break. More."

"If so . . ."

"NO. FRIEND NO BREAK!" Asin shoved Daniel.

Again, Lady Nyssa cleared her throat.

"I have to—"

"NO." Tail stuck up directly beneath her, another Adventurer moved towards the pair. The Catkin turned, lightning fast, and snarled at him, her ears going flat against her skull. The man, seeing something wild and untamed in her eyes, backed off.

"Asin, I can't . . ."

The Catkin spun around, hissing at Daniel as he tried to speak.

"Enough!" Lady Nyssa snapped, fed up. The Catkin glared back at her, and facing the untamed wildness in her eyes, almost quailed. Then, she remembered the Royal Bodyguard who would likely see them all in the dungeons, just long enough for the king to send them to the headsmen. But most of all, she recalled the still, pale body of the prince. A man who had fought with them, laughed with them, ate with them.

A party member.

"Enough." Lady Nyssa's voice grew softer as she put a hand on Asin's shoulder. The Catkin pulled away, but it didn't stop the noblewoman's words. "Daniel has to do this. If not, the prince—Roland—will die. He's a friend too, isn't he?"

A reluctant nod. Then, Asin jerked her chin up. "Daniel best."

"He is. A better man than any of us. But he needs to do this. He *wants* to do this." She jerked her chin to Daniel who was listening to the pair, his eyes a little distant now. Lost, again, somewhere. "Let him."

"Broken." Asin's voice was softer now.

"Then we'll pick up the pieces. But he has to do this. For us." Mulish, but softening. "For Roland." Asin's face softened even further, the bonds of companionship showing. "For himself."

And now, those big, jade eyes began to pool with tears.

"Asin." Daniel spoke softly. "Please."

"Fine . . ." The Catkin turned away, and Daniel gave her back a sad smile. Then, the man straightened and turned, walking towards the wooden doorway in front of which the Royal Bodyguards stood. To where Roland lay, tended by Healers who scrambled to save him.

Lady Nyssa watched, and if there were tears in her eyes too, well, she was not ashamed of them.

Chapter 17

Daniel exhaled, his hand hovering over the still form of the prince. He was laid on the bed in the center of the room, Healers hovering around him and muttering at one another. Many looked pale, the consequence of pouring all their Mana into the patient. And perhaps, worry too.

He had heard some of the conversation as he went in, while waiting for Asin to be convinced. How this was not the only attack, how a number of others had been attacked. No other royalty, but enough to weaken the royal family. A political play, not a civil war. Brad was saved that, at the least.

Not that it mattered to Roland.

Daniel had so few memories of the man. Mostly brief flashes. He had so few memories at all. He had spent some time, while eating, while resting looking at his character sheet. He was down to below Level 10—a pitiful Level-9 Adventurer. His Miner Level was a 2. So many of his skills had dropped too. And outside of that, outside of his attributes . . .

His childhood, his teenage years, the last few years fighting. It was so spotty. Men, women, acquaintances. All of it, faded. He had half conversations, quarters of them.

He had lost a lot. Too much. And glowing, the last notification that he had not closed as yet, stared before him.

WARNING! Martyr's Gift has been overused in a short period.
Permanent and irreversible damage may occur if use of Martyr's Gift continues.

"Are you going to do anything or just stare?" the Royal Bodyguard, the leader, snarled.

Daniel turned his head and just stared at the man, a little bit of the frustration and anger that he was feeling leaked out. At first the bodyguard stared back, but eventually he ducked his head.

"Sorry. I just . . . please. Save him."

Daniel turned away, sighing. In truth, he knew he had been delaying. He let his hand land on the prince's bare shoulder. He paused, looking up at the others and spoke softly. "If this goes bad . . . tell them . . . tell Asin . . . thanks."

The bodyguard nodded.

Then, Daniel tapped into his Gift for the final time and dove within the prince's body to fix him. Knowing he would give whatever it took, to fix the man.

No matter the price.

Chapter 18

Omrak tugged on his neck, the high collared coat and tunic beneath uncomfortably tight and restrictive. Court fashion had kept to its love for tight clothing, for which the extra tight breeches and codpiece ensemble was certainly unflattering to many. Not for Omrak of course, but for other smaller Southeners, it seemed a foolish thing to wear.

Then again, Southerners were very foolish. Look at this entire tragedy, the way it had impacted his friend and the prince. It was not even to take over the kingdom—the royal family was too secure for that—but to gain a minor advantage.

Fools.

He had done his best to avoid getting involved in the discussions, playing the uncultured and foolish Northerner. Unfortunately, he had played it all too well. Too many nobles and Adventurers felt it safe to discuss politics within hearing range of himself, and even if he had wanted to avoid it, lessons from Lady Nyssa had permeated his consciousness.

As such, he knew of the retaliatory attacks. The use of the royal family's Daggers, the sudden rash of suicide among certain noble families. Suicide by strangulation, poison, and disemboweling. Very painful ways to go, all of them. Obviously the shame had taken them.

Obviously.

Rather than dwell on that, Omrak turned to look at his team. Everyone else was here, dressed up in well-fitting clothing and looking much more at ease. Even Asin looked comfortable in the clothing she wore—and what a scandal that had been, when the Royal Tailor himself had taken time out of his busy schedule to work on her clothes. It seemed he had meant to make a statement, since no Beastkin had ever been invited to the court in this way.

Statement was definitely the thing. Her entire ensemble was green and gold, with the gold dominating her dress, tunic combination. The entire thing was body hugging, emphasizing her thin and svelte figure without actually hiding it, with carefully placed cutouts and lacing doing the job. The entire clothing ensemble emphasized her Beastkin nature and her stark beauty.

As for the others—well, Johan looked put together as he always did, though his mother hovered around him, pulling and prodding at his clothing. Quite unmanly, to be primped at so much, but the nature of parent and children's relationships was not something Omrak intended to discuss.

Nor was he getting involved in the entire thing going on between Charles and Lady Nyssa. Matters between the pair had grown tense since Charles's near death and his forced retirement as her bodyguard. The fact that he had been forced out of her service but promptly applied for a spot on the team as an individual had caused quite the friction. It still had yet to be resolved since their erstwhile team leader was . . .

Well.

"Remember, when the horns blow you should . . ."

"I know," Daniel said, snapping at the protocol officer standing beside him, reiterating the ritual they were forced to memorize multiple times already. "I forgot everything that happened before, not everything ever. I'm not stupid."

"Of course not . . . uh . . . Adventurer." The officer sketched another bow, this time lower.

Daniel glared and then turned away, and if Omrak was the only one who saw the flash of irritation give way to sudden sympathy and a deeper fear, he was not about to tell anyone. He understood Daniel's feelings, a little at least. Coming down South, being trapped in a place that was new and different, without the moorings of the familiar had been hard for him.

How much harder was it for Daniel, who had lost so much of who he had been? He was barely a Level 3 Adventurer now, all his Levels in Miner gone. He had a pair of Healing spells left and a smattering of other skills. All his hard-won work . . . gone.

Along with memories of smaller, lesser things. Like faces, names, social incidents. The first few weeks after he had finished healing the prince and had collapsed had been tough. A strong man, thrown into confusion, fear, and anger constantly as he faced a world and a mind that made little sense.

It had been hard, for Omrak and the team, for the Healers and nurses that worked with the ex-Healer, till he had gained some modicum of balance. If anything, Daniel should still be there, in that small compound, relearning the extent of his memory losses—reading, talking, socializing, and training slowly.

Not here, being paraded around by the royal family.

But what did he know? He was just a dumb Northerner.

Horns sounded, the doors were thrown open and the group announced. And once more, their team was put on stage.

Hopefully for the last time.

***

"... and for sacrificing his Erlis-given Gift for my son's sake, we bestow upon Daniel Chai, Adventurer, the rank of baron, to be passed down along his lineage forevermore. During his lifetime, we too waive all taxes on his holdings and furthermore, grant him a stipend from the Crown of five hundred Platinum pieces a year and the usage of one of our Stewards in the running of his holdings, for we are informed the Adventurer shall continue his duties, cleansing our lands of the taint of Ba'al."

The man droned on and on, though Daniel barely heard him. Not since the first line. Not man. King. It didn't matter; it was all the same to him. Oh, he understood he was supposed to care about his station, about the fact that he could kill him or that he ruled over everyone but . . .

It was all so pedestrian.

He had stripped himself of his own memory, sacrificed a Gift that supposedly had made him the most powerful Healer in the entirety of the land. What could a little threat of death and dismemberment mean to him after that?

Anyway, most people were fine if he was a little more irate, a little more distracted than he actually was. They were willing to make excuses for how he acted, what he remembered or when he broke a social cue. They were willing to make a lot of excuses.

Too bad he wasn't.

It would be a lot simpler then, to not get frustrated over being so far behind everyone else. To wake up, day in and day out, with notifications constantly plaguing his day as he gained all those easy skills and skill levels that everyone else had taken for granted as kids.

Easier to forget about that single, broken notification that he had yet to minimize.

Gift: Martyr's Sacrifice Lost
Damage sustained to memories and Gift too great. Loss of Gift has been enacted to preserve soul of user.

And the one after that.

Hidden Quest Achieved: Make Use of My Gift Properly
Reward: (Unknown)

He had told others of the first notification. It was hard to hide such things and in the first few days of his recovery, he had not even considered that he had anything to hide. All but that last notification. Something deep within him told Daniel that he was to keep that notification to himself. Even the one time he wanted to mention it to Asin, he had felt something press down on his soul, forcing him to stay silent.

"Kneel, Daniel Chai and accept your title."

Daniel blinked, feeling a tiny sharp claw digging into his side, to realize that others were looking at him. He had a vague memory that this was not the first time someone had called him. He stumbled forwards, moving towards where the page indicated and knelt.

Head bowed, Daniel waited as the king descended, drawing the sword from his side. As the man approached, Daniel felt the pressure of the king's aura press upon him, forcing him to clench his jaw. Even retracted, the pressure was too great for him at his current level.

Cold, the steel of the sword was cold against his skin. One shoulder and then the other, words passing over his head, more rhythmic words of ceremony and ostentatiousness. When the sword was pulled back and sheathed, the king spoke again.

"Stand, Lord Chai."

Daniel rose, his head coming up a little to eye the man's doublet. Then, the king spoke, not out of rote, his voice filled with passion.

"Look up. You, of all people, have the right to look at us without fear. You have sacrificed all that we could ask and more, in saving our child."

Daniel raised his gaze slowly, meeting wintry grey eyes. The king smiled and lowered his voice, his next words for Daniel only. Well, Daniel and the Catkin with her extended senses.

"Know that you'll always have a favor owed to you. Ask, if you ever need it."

A bow, a dismissal, and even more words. It took all too long, for a ceremony that Daniel had no desire to be part of. They spoke of sacrifice, of things lost, of saving the prince. And none of it, he could remember. Even if he knew it was him in truth who had done it all, still, he could not help but feel a fake.

After all, he had no memories of any of it.

None at all.

All he had, Daniel realized as he walked out of the reception room was his team, those who had been with him through every step of his recovery. People who, for their own reasons, had stood by him when he had fallen and raised him up, even when he had no desire to rise.

Perhaps he might have no memories, no Gift, no Levels. He might only have the barest knowledge of who and what he had been, but Daniel realized, the man who he had lost, he was a man deserving of respect and loyalty. Who had deserved the prizes and nobility gifted to him.

It seemed to him, as he left with his friends, to a new life, that he had much to live up to.

Luckily, he had a lot of friends who could help him do that.

The End

And that's all, folks. This is the series end! Daniel and team will continue Adventuring, but I don't expect to return to this series anytime soon.

Epilogue

The entrance to the Dungeon looked familiar, in the way certain events might feel like an echo of itself. It made Daniel shake, the strange familiarity that faced him as he stared at the way in. Around him, youngsters—teenagers for the most part—laughed and joked while waiting for the pair of older guards to begin the briefing. More than one shot Daniel a questioning look, more for the quality of his armor and his friends than his age. Or so he presumed.

"You didn't have to come," Daniel said, for the umpteenth time.

"Know. Still here," Asin replied, grinning around the heavily spiced meat roll she was chewing.

"Your first Dungeon delve! How could I miss it, Friend Daniel!" Omrak rumbled.

"I've not done the Karlak Dungeon. It should be interesting," Lady Nyssa murmured.

Charles nodded in agreement. "Very much so."

Daniel let his gaze dart over the group, grinning at him. Johan had wanted to come, but his role as the prince's personal bodyguard would keep him in the capital from now on. The prince himself was no longer allowed to go gallivanting around, Adventuring as he liked. Of them all, it was perhaps Roland whose newly constricted life had suffered the most from the attack. Still, his near death had seemed to settle the prince, leaving him more at peace with his role in the royal family.

"You know, I don't need you to watch over me in a *Beginner Dungeon*," Lady Nyssa hissed at Charles.

A familiar nod. "And I will not be. I am instead gaining my rank the proper way."

"You . . ."

Daniel chuckled a little, listening to the pair bicker. Then, his attention was drawn back, to the pair of guards readying themselves for the speech. He stepped forward, waving goodbye to his friends, watching as Asin gave him a lazy, predatory grin before he was among the crowd of low-level Adventurers.

Adventurers like him who were here to finish their very first Dungeon. To make their way via force of arms, skill, and wit towards fortune and excitement. To cleanse the world of Ba'al's continued taint and to do their duty. To *experience* things.

And he, among them. Just another Adventurer now, just another hopeful fool who had a lot to learn and a lot more to experience.

Though, looking back to see his friends and the blonde elf standing with them, smiling back at him gently, Daniel had to admit: maybe had a few advantages.

Author's Note

And that's the series. Ending with Daniel losing his Gift, becoming what he always wanted to be—just another Adventurer. He never had huge ambitions, never desired to even become a famous Adventurer. He just wanted to see a little more of the world, do a little more than swing a pickaxe at a mine wall. Not that he can remember much of that now, but the impressions remain.

The Adventures on Brad was my first series as an author, and looking at it now, there are numerous issues. The Status Sheets, the layout, and even the worldbuilding leaves something to be desired from my perspective. However, there's a charm to the world too—a simplicity to the stories that range from 40-50,000 words each, meant to encompass a day in the life of a relatively average Adventurer.

I hope you enjoyed the series and the ending. It took a few years to get here since I released book six, but I didn't want to leave you all hanging entirely. So I wrote these last three books hoping to complete Daniel's arc and put him on the path that he has always wanted.

Will he, Asin and Omrak still have more adventures? Undoubtedly. There are always more Dungeons to explore, entire kingdoms they have yet to visit and monsters to battle. But Daniel, as a character, has stabilized. He knows what he wants and for once, there's nothing stopping him from getting it.

Thank you all for reading. I hope that the ending was to your liking.

If you enjoyed what I've written, as always, I have multiple other series to read, including my bestselling xianxia Chinese fantasy series whose first chapter I have attached to the end for your pleasure.

Once again, thanks for joining me on this journey.

Sincerely,

Tao

Please check out my other series. I have written the System Apocalypse (a post-apocalyptic LitRPG), A Thousand Li (a xianxia cultivation story) and the Hidden Wishes (an urban fantasy GameLit). Book one of each series follow:

- **Life in the North**
  (Book 1 of the System Apocalypse)
  https://readerlinks.com/l/976138
- **A Gamer's Wish**
  (Book 1 of the Hidden Wishes series)
  https://books2read.com/gamers-wish
- **A Thousand Li: the First Step**
  (Book 1 of the A Thousand Li series)
  https://readerlinks.com/l/971660

In addition, please take a look at other series/books I have co-written:

- **Leveled up Love!** by Tao Wong & A. G. Marshall
  https://books2read.com/leveled-up-love

- **A Fist Full of Credits** by Tao Wong & Craig Hamilton
  (Book 1 of System Apocalypse: Relentless)
  https://readerlinks.com/l/2179306
- **Town Under** by Tao Wong & K.T. Hanna
  (Book 1 of System Apocalypse: Australia)
  https://readerlinks.com/l/2179307

For more great information about great LitRPG series, check out the Facebook groups:

- GameLit Society
  https://www.facebook.com/groups/LitRPGsociety/

- LitRPG Books
  https://www.facebook.com/groups/LitRPG.books/

About the Author

Tao Wong is an avid fantasy and sci-fi reader who spends his time working and writing in the North of Canada. He's spent way too many years doing martial arts of many forms and having broken himself too often, now spends his time writing about fantasy worlds.

If you'd like to support him directly, Tao now has a Patreon page where previews of all his new books can be found!

- Tao Wong's Patreon
  https://www.patreon.com/taowong

For updates on the series and his other books (and special one-shot stories), please visit the author's website:

https://www.mylifemytao.com

Subscribe to Tao's mailing list to receive exclusive access to short stories in the Thousand Li and System Apocalypse universes.

Or visit Tao's Facebook Page:
https://www.facebook.com/taowongauthor/

About the Publisher

Starlit Publishing is wholly owned and operated by Tao Wong. It is a science fiction and fantasy publisher focused on the LitRPG & cultivation genres. Their focus is on promoting new, upcoming authors in the genre whose writing challenges the existing stereotypes while giving a rip-roaring good read.

For more information on Starlit Publishing, visit our website: https://starlitpublishing.com/

You can also join Starlit Publishing's mailing list to learn of new, exciting authors and book releases.

A Thousand Li: the First Step

Chapter 1

"Cultivation, at its core, is a rebellion."

Waiting for their reaction, the thin, mustached older teacher stared at the students seated cross-legged before him. Apparently not seeing the reaction he wanted, the teacher flung the long, trailing sleeves of the robes he wore with a harrumph and continued his lecture. Keeping his expression entirely neutral, Long Wu Ying could not help but smirk within. Such a statement, no matter how contentious, lost its impact after daily repetition over the course of a decade.

"Cultivation demands one to defy the very heavens itself. Each step on the path of cultivation sets you on the road to rebellion to defy the heavens, to defy our king. It is only by his good graces and his belief in the betterment of the kingdom that you are allowed to cultivate."

Wu Ying struggled to keep his face neutral as the refrain continued. Usually, he could tune out the teacher until it came time to cultivate, but today he struggled to do so. Today, he could not help but rebut the teacher in his mind. Teaching the villagers how to cultivate was a purely practical decision on the king's part. Most children would achieve at least the first level of Body Cleansing by their twelfth birthday. That allowed them to grow stronger and healthier, even on the little food they had left after the state, the nobles, and the sects had taken their portion.

"The beneficent auspices of the king allow you to cultivate, study the martial arts, and defend yourself. It is only because of his belief that each village must be a strong member of the kingdom that we have grown to the heights we have!"

It had nothing to do with the desire to begin training the villagers to be useful soldiers in the never-ending wars. Or to ensure that the village was not robbed of the grain they farmed by the bandits that seemed to grow in number every year. Or the fact that less than two hundred li[1]

---

[1] Half a kilometer or roughly a third of a mile

away, the Verdant Green Waters Sect watched over them all, searching for new recruits.

"Now, begin!"

Exhaling a grateful breath that Master Su had finally finished, Wu Ying tried to focus his mind on cultivating. That he respected his teacher was without question, but Master Su was a stickler for the rules, which required him to give the same lecture every single time. Even a saint would find it hard to listen after a while. And Wu Ying was many things, but a Saint he most definitely was not.

It didn't help that the state was obviously of two minds about cultivation itself. The three pillars of a kingdom were the government, the populace, and the cultivating sects. A weakness in any of the three would make a kingdom vulnerable. For a kingdom to be stable, each pillar needed to be as strong, as upright and firm, as the others. If any single pillar grew too high, it would eventually lead to the collapse of the kingdom.

Because of that, a wise ruler would support the development of their populace through cultivation, the surest and best form of developing an individual. But a single cultivator, if they achieved true power, could—and had, historically—overturn governments. And so, the state would always view cultivators and cultivation with some degree of distrust.

"Wu Ying. Focus!" Master Su said.

Wu Ying grimaced slightly before he made his face placid again. Master Su was right. He could think about all these thoughts another time. This was the time for cultivation. The time a villager had to cultivate was limited and precious. Stray thoughts were wasteful.

Drawing a deep breath, Wu Ying exhaled through his nose. The first step in cultivation was to clear the mind. The second was to control his breathing, for breath was the source of all things. At least in the Yellow Emperor's Cultivation Method that had been passed down and used by all peasants in the kingdom of Shen.

The first step on the road to cultivation was that of bodily purification. To ascend, to gain greater strength and develop one's chi, a cultivator needed to purify their body of the wastes that accumulated. Starting the process young helped to reduce the amount of such waste build up and speeded up the progress of cultivation. That was why every villager began cultivating as soon as possible. Those children who achieved the first level of Body Cleansing at a young age were hailed as prodigies.

Wu Ying was not considered a prodigy. Wu Ying had started cultivating at the age of six, like every other child in the village, and through hard work and discipline, he'd managed to achieve not just the first level of Body Cleansing but the second. True prodigies, at Wu Ying's age of seventeen, would already be at the fourth or fifth stage. Each of the twelve stages of Body Cleansing saw the conscious introduction and cleansing of another major chi meridian. When an individual had consciously introduced and could control the flow of chi through all twelve major pathways, all the stages of Body Cleansing were considered complete.

Wu Ying breathed in then out, slowly and rhythmically. He focused on the breath, the flow of air into his lungs, the way it entered his body as his stomach expanded and his chest filled out. Then he exhaled, feeling his stomach contract, the diaphragm moving upward as air circulated away.

In time, Wu Ying moved his focus away from breathing toward his dantian. Located below his belly button, in the space just slightly below his hip line and a few inches beneath the surface of his body, the lower dantian was the core of the Yellow Emperor's Cultivation Method. From there, through the flow and consolidation of one's internal chi, one would progress.

Once again, Wu Ying felt the mass of energy that was his dantian. As always, it was large in size but low in density, uncompacted and diffuse. His job was to gently nudge the flow of energy through his body's meridians, to send it on a major circulation through his body. In the process, his body sweated, as the normally docile chi moved through his body, cleansing and scouring away the impurities of life. In time, Wu Ying's normal sweat mixed with the impurities in his body, flowing from his pores. The rancid, bitter odor from Wu Ying's body mixed with the similar pungence coming from the rest of the class, a stench that even the open windows of the building could do little to disperse.

***

Deep in the process of cultivating, none of the students noticed the rancid smell, leaving only Master Su to suffer as he watched over the teenagers. Master Su had long gotten used to the offensive odor that he would be forced to endure for the next few hours as each of the classes progressed. It was a fair trade though, for Master Su received ten tael[2] of silver and, most importantly, a Marrow Cleansing pill each month for his work.

Deep in their cultivation, none of the students moved when a young man shook and convulsed. But Master Su took action, flashing over to the boy with a tap of his foot. Paired fingers raised as Master Su studied the thrashing boy before they darted forward, striking in rapid succession a series of acupressure points along the body. After the third strike, the convulsing

---

[2] A measurement of weight. Roughly 37.5 grams

slowed then stopped before the boy tipped over, coughing out blood.

"Foolish. Pushing to open the second meridian channel when you have not finished cleansing the first!" Master Su berated the boy, shaking his head. "Get up. Begin cultivating properly. You will stay here an extra hour."

"But…" the boy protested weakly but quieted at Master Su's glare.

"Foolish child!" Master Su growled as he stomped back to his station in front of the class. If he had not been there, the boy would likely have damaged himself permanently. Master Su watched as the boy wiped his mouth clear of blood before he snorted. Luckily, Master Su had been able to quell the rampaging chi flow, but the boy would likely have to spend the next few weeks on light duty at his farm. A bad time for that, considering the planting season they were in. "Stupid."

As the hour set aside for the teenagers to cultivate came to an end and the morning sun cast long shadows on the small village, the village bell rang. Master Su frowned slightly then smoothed his face as the students broke free from their cultivation trances one by one. It would never do for the students to see his concern.

"The session is over. Line up when you are done," Master Su commanded before he walked out of the small, single-room building that made up his school.

Outside, the teacher walked forward slightly, turning his head from side to side before he spotted the growing dust cloud.

"Master Su." Tan Cheng, the tall village head, came up to Master Su.

As the two individuals in the sixth level of the Body Cleansing stage, the pair shared the burden of guarding the village from external threats. It helped that Chief Tan was a lover of tea like Master Su.

"Chief Tan," Master Su greeted. "What is it?"

"The army recruiters," Chief Tan said, his eyes grave.

Master Su could not help but wince. This was the third time in as many years that the army had recruited from their village. The conscripts from the first year had yet to return, though news of deaths had trickled back. The war between their state of Shen and the state of Wei had dragged on, bringing misery to everyone.

"They're going to raise the taxes again then," Master Su said, trying to keep his tone light. Each year that the war dragged on, the taxes grew higher. He wondered how many the army would take this time and did not envy his friend. The first time the army arrived, they had filled the requirements with volunteers. The second time they came, each household that had more than one son and had yet to send a volunteer had sent their sons. This time, there would be no easy choices.

"Most likely." Chief Tan chewed on his lip slightly. As the rest of the villagers slowly streamed in from the surrounding fields, he looked around then looked down, avoiding the expectant gazes of the parents. Whatever came next, few would be happy.

***

"What is it?" Qiu Ru asked. The raven-haired beauty of the class prodded Wu Ying in the back as she tried to peer past the crowd of students who had gathered around the windows. Giving up, she prodded Wu Ying once more in the back to get him to answer.

"The army," Wu Ying finally answered.

As her eyes widened, he admired the way it made them shine—before he squashed his burgeoning feelings again. Qiu Ru had made it quite clear last summer festival that she had no interest in him. Now, Wu Ying had his sights set on Gao Yan. Even if Gao Yan was shorter, plumper, and had a bad tendency to forget to brush her teeth. That was life in the village— your choices were somewhat limited.

"Are they bringing back the volunteers?" Qiu Ru said.

"No. They're too early for that," Cheng Fa Hui said.

Wu Ying glanced at his friend, who had hung back with the rest of them. Not that Fa Hui needed to be up front to see what was happening. He towered over the entire group by a head. All except Wu Ying, who only lost to him by a handbreadth.

"If the army was returning our people, it would be before the winter," Fa Hui said. "That way the lord would not need to feed them."

Wu Ying grimaced and shot a look around the room, relaxing slightly when he saw that Yin Xue had not come to class today. As the nearest village to Lord Wen's summer abode, all the villagers dealt with Lord Wen and his son regularly. Truth be told, Yin Xue did not need to come to their village class, but the boy seemed to take pleasure in showcasing his ability over the peasants. As the son of the local lord, Yin Xue had access to a private cultivation tutor, spiritual herbs, and good food—all of which had allowed him to progress to Body Cleansing four already. In common parlance, he was what was known as a false dragon—a "forced" genius, rather than one who had achieved the heights of his cultivation by genius alone.

If Yin Xue had heard Fa Hui... Wu Ying mentally shuddered at the thought. Still, it was not as if Fa Hui was wrong. If the war was over, it made sense to make the villagers feed the returned sons rather than pay for hungry mouths over the winter.

"Are they here for us then?" Wu Ying mused. That would make sense.

After saying the words out loud, he noticed how the rest of the class stiffened. Before he could say anything to comfort them, Master Su called them out of the building.

Once the students had lined up outside, Wu Ying could easily see the army personnel, two of which were speaking with Chief Tan, while the others watched over the conscripts. As it was still early in the morning, the army had only managed to visit one other village thus far, and as such, there were only twenty such conscripts standing together. Yin Xue sat astride a horse, beside the conscripts but not part of them.

Wu Ying had to admit, the members of the army looked dashing in their padded undercoats, dark lamellar armor, and open-faced helms. But having watched two other groups leave and not return, with only rumors of the losses trickling back via the same recruiters and the itinerant merchant, much of the prestige and glory of joining the army had faded.

"Men, Lord Wen has sent his men to us once again. We are required to send twenty strong conscripts to join the king's army this year." Before the crowd could grasp the significance of the number, Chief Tan announced, "All sons from families who have not sent a child to the front, step forward."

Wu Ying stepped forward. As the only surviving son of his family, he had been safe from the recruiters beforehand. Along with Wu Ying, another six men stepped forward.

"All sons from families with more than one son in the village, step forward," Chief Tan announced.

This time, there was some confusion, but it was soon sorted out with some students pushed forward and others drawn back. By now, Wu Ying counted seventeen "volunteers."

"Why not daughters?" Qiu Ru called.

Wu Ying could not help but grimace at her impertinent words. As the local beauty, Qiu Ru had managed to get away with more impertinent comments than others. Interrupting the Chief while he was speaking was a new high.

"The army is looking for men!" Chief Tan snapped. "Qiu Jan! See to your daughter!"

"This is foolish!" Qiu Ru said.

When Chief Tan began to speak, he was silenced by a raised hand of the lieutenant, whose gaze raked over Qiu Ru. "You are quite the beauty. But our men do not need wives."

The hiss from the crowd was loud even as Qiu Ru flushed bright red at the insult.

"We are here to find soldiers. And you are, what? Body Cleansing one? Women are no use to us as soldiers until at least Body Cleansing four!"

Still flushed, Qiu Ru moved to speak, but her mother had managed to make her way over to the impertinent girl and gripped her arm. With a yank of her hand, the mother pulled Qiu Ru back. For a time, the lieutenant looked over the group, seeing that no one else was liable to interrupt, before he looked at Chief Tan.

"Tan Fu, Qiu Lee, Long Mao. Join the others," Chief Tan said softly.

Everyone knew why he had chosen the three, of course. Their families had been gifted with more than three surviving sons. Even now, their parents would have a single son left to work the farm, turn the earth. A good thing. Better than the families that were left without any. If you didn't consider the fact that now, three of their sons were fighting a war that none of them ever wanted.

"Good," the lieutenant said as his gaze slid over the new conscripts.

Wu Ying looked to the side as well, offering Fa Hui a tight smile as he saw his big friend look sallow and scared.

"Conscripts, return to your homes and collect your belongings. You will not be back for many months. Bring what you need. We will march in fifteen minutes. Gather at first bell," the lieutenant said.

The students stared at one another, looking at the few members of the class that were left, then at the other children. Wu Ying sighed and clapped Fa Hui on the shoulder, giving the giant a slight shove to send him toward his family. As if the motion was a signal, the group broke apart, the teenager's faces fixed as they moved to say their final goodbyes.

Read more of A Thousand Li: The First Step
https://readerlinks.com/l/1340822

Made in the USA
Las Vegas, NV
20 April 2022

47776346R00174